GOD'S UNWAVERING PROMISES

A STORY OF RADICAL FAITH

Phyllis J. Ryser

Author's Tranquility Press
ATLANTA, GEORGIA

Copyright © 2024 by Phyllis J. Ryser

All rights reserved. No part of this publication may be reproduced, distributed or transmitted in any form or by any means, including photocopying, recording, or other electronic or mechanical methods, without the prior written permission of the publisher, except in the case of brief quotations embodied in critical reviews and certain other noncommercial uses permitted by copyright law. For permission requests, write to the publisher, addressed "Attention: Permissions Coordinator," at the address below.

Phyllis J. Ryser/Author's Tranquility Press
3900 N Commerce Drive, Suite 300 #1255
Atlanta, GA 30344
www.authorstranquilitypress.com

Ordering Information:
Quantity sales. Special discounts are available on quantity purchases by corporations, associations, and others. For details, contact the "Special Sales Department" at the address above.

God's Unwavering Promises: A Story of Radical Faith/Phyllis J. Ryser
Paperback: 978-1-959930-45-7
eBook: 978-1-959930-46-4

Contents

Chapter 1: A Solemn Pledge 7

Chapter 2: The Magical Experience 22

Chapter 3: The Priest, The Pharaoh, and their Plot 30

Chapter 4: The Dreadful Proposition 41

Chapter 5: Doubt and Fear 57

Chapter 6: The Late-Night Tragedy 67

Chapter 7: Unwitting Collaboration 78

Chapter 8: Red Paint on the Gate and the Soothsayer's Warning 85

Chapter 9: Unholy Sacrifice and the Horrific Day of Sorrow 95

Chapter 10: The Prophecy and a Message from the Starry Sky 106

Chapter 11: A Divine Blessing and Resolute Determination 114

Chapter 12: The Dismal Princess and an Overheard Conversation 124

Chapter 13: Deception and Discovery 132

Chapter 14: The Daring Scheme 143

Chapter 15: Doubt, Fear and Anger 152

Chapter 16: Reconciliation and Hope 159

Chapter 17: Preparing For A New Adventure 172

Chapter 18: The Final Journey 177

Epilogue 182

References 187

Questions for Discussion 193

A Note from the Author 195

Jochebed on her wedding day

Chapter 1:
A Solemn Pledge

"I am God Almighty, walk before me, and be blameless. And I will make my covenant between me and you and will multiply you exceedingly,"
Genesis 17:1-2

Jochebed struggles to heave the heavy rock onto the growing pile. As the rock leaves her hands its sharp edges scrape away her skin and bring blood. She ignores the pain and grabs her scarf as it starts to slide too far off her head. Mother's admonition rings in her ears, "Remember. Never let them see your face or your hair."

The young girl pulls the cloth over her dark hair before the sun can ignite the auburn shine in the wavy tresses. Sweat drips from her hairline and trickles down her forehead, but she lowers the cloth over her eyebrows and pulls the neckwrap over her nose. With only her eyes uncovered, she looks toward the chariot where a man wearing a helmet is standing surveying the work site. Two men in loincloths stand on the ground, arms folded, and a leather whip dangling from their hand. They keep a close watch on the women wearing drab head wraps and tunics who are scouring the ground for rocks, like a flock of hungry brown hens feeding in a field where grain has been harvested.

Jochebed stoops to pick up a large stone when one of the men turns toward her. From the corner of her eye, she watches him until she is sure he has turned away. Breathing a sigh of relief, she continues to gather up the rocks and toss them on the heap.

A fellow laborer moves closer toward her. Stooping to the ground, Jochebed pretends to be digging up a rock. She waits for the person who is nearing her to speak.

"Jocki, are you excited about your wedding?" The question comes in a whisper.

Jochebed looks closely into the eyes peering at her from under layers of thin cloth. "Ana?"

"Ha!" Ana laughs, "I knew you from the way you moved. And I know you never mistake my green eyes. Relax. It is only me."

"Yes. Your green eyes give you away every time. The thought of my wedding is exciting but also a little scary. It will be a big change. I hope to do well as a wife. Thinking of myself as a wife feels strange to me."

"I am excited as well!" Ana says, "I get to be a bridesmaid! Thank you for asking me. It is going to be the biggest celebration I can remember. I can't wait to dance. It has been so long since we have had anything to celebrate. Your wedding is all the talk in the village. I want time to enjoy a feast and some fun for a few days. It is so much fun to celebrate with all the families. I wish we could do it more often. Celebrations seem to give everyone a lift in spirit. We need more hope for our future and a reason for our hard work."

Keeping an eye on the men at the edge of the site, they pause their dialogue at intervals to disguise their conversation. Lingering too long without putting rocks on the pile could give away their communications.

"You are right about needing more time to celebrate with our family. Father planned the wedding on the day of the Dog Star Festival so the Egyptians would be so drunk with celebrating their holidays that they wouldn't care what Israelites did during that time. They would kill us with work if they didn't take time off for themselves to party and celebrate their gods."

"That's so true. Their idols keep them busy and drunk. By the way, what is Abahail saying about your wedding?" Ana asks, curiously.

"I don't know. Her opinions are not my concern. She has never said a kind word to Mother or me so I avoid her and Orpha in every way I can. She is like the donkey who brays loudly before dawn because she is hungry, but when you bring her some straw, she bites your arm."

Ana laughs her characteristic chuckle. "She-ass is a good description of her. What has your father said about her sons? Everyone I know says they are very angry that he is giving you in marriage to Amram."

"Father has not said anything about them, but he seems a little worried. He will not say anything in my presence because he just wants me to be happy about my wedding. He keeps saying he plans to anoint Amram as the leader soon, but I do not know if it will be at the wedding. I hope so because it would make Amram happy and settle a lot of uncertainty."

Ana muses. "That anointing could stir a rift within the tribe. Amram is popular with the people, so he may be able to handle any trouble those rogues may make. I hope Amram is ready to face trouble."

Eager to change the subject Jochebed says, "Father has arranged for me to wear a beautiful dress like our ancient mothers wore when they married the tribal leader. I can't wait to see it. I will feel very honored to wear such a dress."

"Huh. That is not surprising. You are Kohath's youngest, and it is no secret you are his favorite. He won't spare anything for your wedding."

Suddenly, loud piercing screams send shockwaves in the air. All the workers stand erect and search for the source of the clamor. An Egyptian taskmaster stands over a woman with his whip raised to strike another blow at her. The woman is on her knees covering her head with her arms and screaming through sobs, begging for the blows to stop. As her screams become louder, he lowers his whip and walks away looking back cursing her as he goes.

Ana and Jochebed remain silent and move away from each other. The scene is all too familiar. A taskmaster's anger may be aroused because he judges a worker to be moving too slowly or spending too much time talking to others, but anyone who draws his attention could be his next victim. The women must endure this day after day during the building seasons. They wait impatiently for any relief from the hard, grueling work and the cruel treatment, but there seems to be no end.

Weeks later when the smell of beer wafting from the Egyptian towns signals the festival of the Dog Star is nearing, Amram has finished his preparations for his wedding to Jochebed.

The long-awaited day has arrived. Amram scrutinizes the small room closely. This room is part of the addition to his widowed mother's house where he has lived from birth. These new quarters will be for himself and his bride. The living area is separated from the rest of the house by goat hair blankets that cover the door to the adjoining space. The prospective groom crosses his whip-lashed scarred arms. He smiles with satisfaction. Mahala, his mother, and his sister Sarah have supplied new blankets, baskets, and cooking utensils to welcome the new bride. Everything looks complete.

Like many of the mudbrick homes in Goshen, the living area is three small rooms. The main entrance to the house has a raised threshold to prevent blowing sand from collecting around the walls. An enclosed courtyard surrounds the house. Cooking and eating areas are in this courtyard where much of the daily work takes place. The family's stock of animals and fowls wander around the yard.

The primary sleeping quarters are on the roof unless the weather prohibits it. The mud brick construction provides a cool interior during the day, but after sundown, the night air is much cooler and more comfortable for sleeping. A reed canopy provides some shade on the roof for activities such as spinning or weaving cloth.

Amram is distracted from his inspection by the sound of men's loud laughter coming from the courtyard. His friends are arriving to accompany him in the groom's procession to the house of the bride's father. From the sounds, many men are coming to support him. He feels grateful for their loyalty and encouragement.

Strapping on his short, curved sword, he reaches for his dagger as he heads to the courtyard. The men greet him with friendly shouts as they gather around with rowdy congratulations. He returns their greetings and thanks each of them for coming.

Seeing Benaiah, his most trusted friend, Amram asks, "Is everything ready to go? Are all the men armed and ready?"

"We are ready when you are. You must be expecting trouble," says Beniah.

"Maybe. I'm hoping my grandfather will anoint me as tribal leader tonight at my wedding. I want to be ready for anything. As you know my uncles are very hostile to this anointing. Grandfather said a year ago he would anoint me, but he is still delaying. I'm wondering if my uncles are pressuring him to change his mind. I just do not want any nasty surprises in case he does announce my anointing. We must be ready for anything," Amram says with seriousness.

Beniah raises his sword as he says, "Whatever happens let it come. We are ready."

"Then let's go, Ben, my friend. I have waited too long to claim my bride."

As the groom's party approaches Kohath's house, excited children scurry back and forth shouting, "He's coming! He's coming!" They run to the gate hoping to see the bridegroom. Each one wants the honor of opening the gate. Tambourines, flutes, and trumpets sound joyous music as the bridegroom and his party approach. Relatives and guests move toward the gate straining to catch a glimpse of the troop.

In the house Hogla, the younger wife of Kohath, pulls the door open just enough to see through a small crack. Turning to address Jochebed she says softly, "I think he may be coming. It is time for you to go to meet him. I was hoping he wouldn't come so early. I wanted you to be with me a few more minutes."

Jochebed goes to the door to peek out. "Let me see what is happening."

Hogla grabs her sixteen-year-old daughter and holds her tightly, as tears stream down her face. "You have been my sunshine and my joy. What will I do now? How can I let you go?"

"Mother, I will be living just a short distance on the other side of this village. You will see me very often. I am not going to leave you. You may come to visit when I am not working in the fields. I will make sure to see you often." Jochebed squeezes her mother tightly. Then releases her.

"I know you will find happiness, my daughter. Amram is strong and kind. You will be safe with him. I do not intend to be so soppy, but I will miss you terribly." She sniffs. "I am very happy for you. I wish I could have been so happy…" She bites her lip to stop the words. Drawing a deep breath, then releasing a sigh.

"I must go to see if your father needs me." Her voice trails away. She lets go of her daughter and slips out to the courtyard.

Jochebed peeks out the door to see what is happening outside. Raising her hands to either side of her face, she exclaims in a jumble of sentences, "I do not know if I can go out in front of so many people. All of them will be looking at me. Why is he coming so early? It is only twilight. I did not expect him to come so early."

Her cheeks turn from pink to red as she paces back and forth across the floor. The beaded strands adorning her headband swing in time with the swishes of her elaborately embroidered skirt. Judith, Ana, and Tirzah, the bride's childhood friends whom she chose as her bridal attendants, gather around her to admire her specially designed wedding dress.

"Father said this dress is like the wedding dresses worn by the brides of our tribal leaders of past generations. Do you think Rebecca wore one that looked like this when she married Isaac?"

She pirouettes holding up the skirt so others can see the richly decorated linen from every angle.

Ana rolls her eyes. "Few women get to wear this kind of elaborate dress. Most of us do not have such indulgent fathers. Often fathers are interested only in the number of goats of cattle or the amount of money the groom can afford to pay him for a bride price. But there are some girls who just happen to be born lucky." She presses her lips together making her chin wrinkle.

"You have the most beautiful dress, and you are going to marry a very handsome, strong man. What are you so nervous about? If you do not go out this door, I will go for you," Judith says twirling a scarf.

"When Jacob thought he was marrying Rachel, he was tricked into marrying Leah instead. Do you think Amram will notice if I cover my face and go out to meet him?" Judith laughs as she snatches Jochebed's bridal veil from its hanger on the wall and puts it over her head.

"I am sure he will notice. You cannot get away with that," Ana says in a sassy tone as she places a scarf over her own face, mimicking Judith. "After all, his eyes have always been only on Jochebed."

"You have already had your own wedding, Judith. You can't steal mine. Give me my veil," Jochebed says impatiently. She takes the veil and drapes it around her shoulders.

Tirzah approaches Jochebed and gently takes her hand. "I wish you very much happiness, my dearest friend. I know you will be happy. We all know Amram is truly kind and honest. He will treat you kindly. Caleb always treats me very well. It is comforting to be with a good man."

"Thank you, Tirzah. I know you have been my dearest friend. You make me happy to be getting married today. You have always been here for me."

The outside noise grows significantly louder. The Shofar, or ram's horn, announces the arrival of the groom's party. Shouts and boisterous laughter drown out the music. Amram has arrived accompanied by his troop of rowdy, young groomsmen who have already caught the smell of wine and beer. With six of his selected companions, Amram enters the courtyard amid cheers from the crowd.

Benaiah marches beside the bridegroom. The seven men, armed with swords swinging from the belt and daggers in leather sheaths strapped to the left arm, come striding across the yard and halt at the center.

As Jochebed and her companions appear a path opens for the bridal train. When the young bride comes near her groom, she bows low to the ground. He smiles and extends his hand. His strong work-worn hand covers hers as he lifts her up to stand by his side. The party moves toward the sycamore tree that serves as Kohath's place of conducting business and handing down his judgments. A ram skin placed on a stone bench is his throne.

Kohath's form is so fragile it seems as if a gust of desert wind could send him rolling over the sand dunes. In years past he was strong and robust until brutal work on Pharaoh's building projects, the lashes from whips of the Egyptian task masters and a hip injury took their toll on his body. Since his injury, he has slowly weakened in his body but not in his iron-willed spirit and unrelenting faith in the God of his ancestors, whom he fervently serves.

Seated on the left of Kohath are his three stony-faced sons, Isher, Hebron, and Ussiel, who wait in silence with their hands hidden under their robes.

When Amram moves toward the trio, he looks at each one with a clear unflinching gaze. "Good evening, gentlemen. How are my favorite uncles getting along?"

They acknowledge him with a curt nod as their lips curl into a snarl. They growl mumbled sounds from the sides of their mouth that are supposed to represent greetings.

"I bid you all sound health and good cheer." The right side of Amran's mouth lifts into a half smile as he turns away from them toward Kohath.

Torchlight bounces off the peeling limestone wall of the mudbrick house illuminating Kohath's frail, withering form. A staff made of olive wood leans against his bench. His white beard and rough-woven linen robes glow softly in the flickering torch light making the seated figure appear as a sculpture molded from clay.

As the couple approaches him, his thin, cracked lips pull back in a smile crinkling the papyrus paper's rough cheeks, revealing brown, worn teeth. The old gentleman is very pleased. His pleasure ignites sparks of excitement and makes him talkative.

"Greetings, my son," Kohath says as the couple comes within his range of vision. "You have made me very happy by choosing this beautiful bride. She will bring you joy as she becomes your faithful wife."

"Greetings to you, Grandfather," Amram responds as he bends to kiss the old man on both cheeks. "I am honored to marry this beautiful woman."

"You are a good and honest man. I am trusting you to continue my mission, given to me by the Almighty. It will be your duty to protect the promise made to Abraham our father when I must sleep with my ancestors."

"You have honored me. When the time comes, I will lead our people on the right path. I have received very good training from you. Thank you for trusting me with this most sacred commission. You are my constant guide."

"I am sure you will honor your mission when your time comes." Smiling broadly, Kohath nods. "May God's blessings be on you, my son.

Kohath produces a small box and opens it. A beautiful bracelet made of hammered gold and copper inlaid with jewels shines from the box. Turning to Jochebed he says, "A bracelet such as this one was presented to our ancient mother, Rebekah, when she agreed to marry our father, Isaac. It is a symbol of our heritage. Do not forget the solemn promises made by our God to our people, my daughter. These promises belong to us as well."

The deep wrinkles crease his rough cheeks as the old chief breaks into a broader smile. He gently puts the bracelet on her wrist and gestures with his long bony finger. Jochebed kneels to receive the blessing. His pale hand trembles slightly as it rests on his young daughter's soft dark hair.

Reciting in his slow, deliberate way, Kohath recites the familiar blessing. *"May your sons increase to thousands upon thousands, and may your children possess the gates of their enemies. Your sons will be mighty in the sight of God. May the favor of the God of our fathers, Abraham, Isaac, and Jacob, rest on you."* He pauses, waiting for her response.

"Yes, Father," she whispers, "I will bless you with many children."

"Your duty and honor, my dear child, is to participate in the promise. Bear healthy, strong children. Guard them carefully. Teach them to hold on to the promise."

Jochebed feels the intensity of her father's admonition. Lifting her head to see his face, her eyes look directly into his. The amber flecks in her hazel eyes dance as her full lips open slightly.

"I will, Father. I will keep the promise."

Kohath smiles and nods his approval. For a moment he contemplates her answer. His frail finger, with strokes as light as a goose feather, touches her smooth cheek. Her words have sealed the promise.

Even though his blessing is finished Kohath continues his speech in his raspy, cracking, sometimes barely audible voice.

The pleasant scent of roasting lamb, fragrant wine and barley beer drifts across the courtyard, mixing with joyful sounds of distant laughter and music. The ringing tambourines beckon Jochebed away from her father's speaking. The sounds of the distant music become louder. The young women are waiting to dance the tribal wedding dances in honor of the bride. Jochebed fidgets trying to keep her eyes on the ground to show respect for her father. Toying with the bracelet, she shifts her body, hoping his speech will end soon. But he continues to speak.

"My time here is short. I have been privileged to tell the account of our fathers for many years. I must remind you once more of the promise from the Almighty."

He stops for a minute to savor the meaning of the story as if he just heard it. Each time he relates the narrative he is more awed by it.

"My ancient father, Abraham, was a Syrian. The Lord Almighty said to him. 'Go to a land I will show you. I will make you a great nation and make your name great. Through you, all the families of the earth will be blessed. Your descendants will be as numerous as the stars in the sky.'" He waves his hand and then points upward to the sky where the stars are beginning to appear. "These very stars are witnesses to this promise. Every time you see them, remember what the Almighty said to our Father."

"Our father believed in Almighty God. He traveled to the land of Canaan. Even though Abraham had no children the Almighty swore to him with an oath that the land would belong to Abraham's descendants. Abraham saw a vision that thousands of his descendants would be slaves in a foreign land. Then the vision revealed to him that after four hundred years all his children would come out of the land with great possessions! They would see a great victory over their oppressors!"

He looks at each person who is near enough for his dim eyes to see. He calls each by name and waits until that person is looking back at him before he continues his speech.

"Abraham's family lived in peace and prosperity in that beautiful land until a famine forced them to go to Egypt and buy food. At first, they were welcomed as friends. Then the Egyptians forgot all they owed to Abraham's family."

Some in his audience are growing impatient with the lengthening speech. But the old one looks at each person to reclaim their attention before continuing.

"Our oppressors hate us and fear us without reason! They make our lives as hard as possible! There is hope if we hold on to the promise of our God! Just as Abraham believed, we must also believe. We will return to our land and live again without oppression! All that the Almighty said would happen is coming true. This is sure evidence His promise is true!"

After a long pause, he takes a deep, loud breath before continuing in a more forceful voice.

"The Almighty said to our father, 'I will bring judgment on the nation where your descendants serve as slaves, and afterward they will come out of the land with great possessions!' Some of you will see your children march out of here to reclaim the sacred land! Our people will not be abandoned to die as slaves forever in this hostile country! We are the Chosen People who will produce the promised Child of Eve! There is hope if we do not lose hope!"

Hogla stands near the wall with her arms crossed tightly under her breasts. She does not intrude within the men's space but stays near enough to see when Kohath motions for her to come to his side. She is rarely far away from her husband. In her fifteenth year, she married Kohath when he was nearing sixty years of age. Now she spends her time dutifully complying with his increasing demands. Her devotion to him is partially due to her respect for him and partially because of fear for her personal safety.

Abahail, Kohath's senior wife, wraps her robe tightly around her bony shoulders and pulls a scarf firmly under her chin. Through narrowed eyes, she studies the wedding couple. Her lips are taut against her teeth. Orpha, her youngest child, a homely, sour-faced girl, huddles close to her mother. Daughters-in-law surrounded by their quiet children sit near on woolen blankets waiting for the speech to end.

Decorum requires everyone to keep silent until Kohath ends his speaking, but Abahail in a stage whisper, nodding toward the bridal couple, spits out words in sharp staccato. Each word ends in a hissing sound like water droplets falling on a hot stone.

Her crooked finger points toward the couple. "Young men are so full of energy and big dreams! Young women are awed by them. See how happy she is! That will change if she does not produce sons soon enough to please him. And just look at that dress and jewelry the old man got for her! The finest linen, jewels, and gold for his favorite daughter! With the Egyptian taxes so high, we can barely afford to eat!"

Motioning her thumb toward her own daughter she says, "Orpha's wedding dress will be a rag compared to this one. Orpha should have been married to Amram four years ago. When is the old man going to choose a husband for her? And just look at that! The girl is looking into his face! He seems pleased with her! Has he forgotten it is not proper for young women to look in the eyes of a tribal chief? The old man is already senile!" She huffs.

Hogla turns her back toward Abahail. She arranges her scarf over her head then pulls it tight over her ears as if to shut out the ranting.

The lines in the Abahail's weathered face become even sharper. Her tone becomes more strident. "I have been a good wife to Kohath all these years. Even though he loved his first wife more I tried with all my strength to please him! He would not even choose one of my sons to be the next tribal leader. It's just not right!"

She blows a forceful breath as she thrusts her hands in her lap. "He said he needed to take a young wife to comfort him in his old age. It is very bitter to be replaced by one so much younger than my own son. He never gave that a thought! He said he was taking a young wife to relieve me of the burden of so much work. Well, the work is not as heavy as the insult!"

Raising her gnarled hands, Abahail looks sharply at Hogla and sees only the back of her head.

"Now he has chosen his youngest daughter to be the wife of the proposed next tribal chief! How much more does he expect me to take? Wasn't Orpha good enough for his favorite grandson? Who will he choose for her? Better her brothers make that choice! And soon! The old man can't live forever. When he is gone, they will see that justice will be done!"

Her mouth snaps shut like the jaws of a crocodile. She sits seething in frustration and bitterness.

Despite the heat from the torches, a cold shudder shakes Hogla's body. Her chest tightens making prickles go up her spine. She draws a few deep breaths. Turning to glance over her shoulder toward her rival she sees Abahail with her jaw clenched, chin thrust forward, glaring toward the bridal couple. A ghost of a smile flits across Hogla's lips. The thought that she now has a strong son-in-law to protect her gives her comfort and a bit of smug satisfaction.

Amram and Jochebed have completed their vows. The bridal party turns to walk away from the old sycamore tree. As they joyfully make their way toward the group of guests who are ready for the celebration, Benaiah touches Amram's shoulder, "Kohath must have suspected trouble would break out and spoil the wedding if he moved to anoint you tonight."

"Looks like it. I have enough to think about tonight. I do not need to fight now. I will just have to be patient a little while longer. My grandfather probably knows best," Amram answers.

"I hope you are right. But this delay is starting to make me nervous. It just gives your uncles more time to plan a revolt. What is Kohath thinking?"

"I'm not sure, but will you be sure to watch my back and listen for any talk from the people? I will talk to all the guys about this as well. We need to be on guard for anything that may happen."

BES, GOD OF THE EGYPTIAN FAMILY

Popular at all levels of Egyptian society, the god Bes was believed to be the protector of the family and particularly newborn children. His image was often carved of wood, painted, and kept in homes to ward off demons.

Chapter 2:
The Magical Experience

"The Lord is in his holy temple; the Lord is on his heavenly throne. He observes the sons of men; his eyes examine them."

Psalms 11:4

Jochebed is grateful her first child is due to come during the season of the river's rising. The Egyptians are preparing for days of feasting; therefore, she along with all Israelites, will enjoy a respite from the grueling toil. For the soon-to-be young mother, it will allow some time to heal from the stresses of childbirth.

The first signs of the impending birth are squeezing sensations in her swollen belly. The nervous anticipation of the birth incites her restlessness as she paces back and forth from room to room.

"You need to take a leisurely walk around the village to enjoy the morning sun. It will help work off the tension and relax your body," Mahala says as she and Sarah are gathering the supplies to prepare the meals for the day.

These two gentle, patient women will be essential to the young mother when the baby arrives since she has had no experience caring for an infant. They have become her confidants and companions. Soon after her wedding, she realized she could depend on them for any advice and help she sought.

"How long do you think it will be before the baby comes?" Jochebed asks.

"That is hard to tell. Your birth signs have only begun. It may be hours, or it could suddenly decide to come quickly. While you wait, you need to relax to allow the body to prepare for a smooth birth. If you are too nervous, you could have more trouble than you should. You need to be ready for the baby's coming," Mahala smiles.

"I will do as you say. You know what to do. I have not been through this. It is exciting but scary," the young woman giggles.

Jochebed goes to her room. She looks around to see if all is ready. For weeks Sarah has helped her plan for the birth. They brought in more blankets and cushions for her comfort and clothes to wrap the child. There are herbs, salt, and pots for the water.

Satisfied, she dons her scarf and leaves the house. As Jochebed steps onto the path, she is greeted with joyful shrieks and shouts from the village children who play in the courtyards. Unhampered by clothes the little boys and girls frolic like the innocent lambs celebrating the new day as if their joy will last forever. Watching them brings the young woman feelings of contentment.

"I know you will run and play in due time, Little One," she says, gently patting her swollen stomach.

An energetic, tousled-haired tot chases his squealing sister with a grasshopper. His impish face, with its mischievous grin, makes Jochebed laugh aloud.

"I can't wait to see you," she says to the moving little treasure inside her body. "Hurry and come quickly. Your Mommy is getting impatient."

Returning to the house after her stroll, she finds Mahala in the back yard grinding wheat for the essential daily bread. After suffering great loss, Mahala has learned to find pearls of joy in daily chores. Her husband's life was lost to the Egyptian work gangs. More tragic losses were heaped on her when her daughter Sarah, lost her husband and children as well.

"The squeezing feelings are coming more often now. They are getting stronger. I just know it must be a boy! Amram will be so pleased if it is a boy. He wants this baby to be his firstborn son to grow up to be head of the tribe. Men always want a boy. If it is a girl, I will not be disappointed.

I cannot wait to see what sort of little person is going to appear!"

Jochebed prattles on as she rubs her belly to feel the movements of the babe inside. She stops her restless pacing and squats beside Mahala. Taking a handful of dough, she pats it into a loaf.

"When I see a ewe give birth, it seems so natural for her. She does not seem to have a bit of trouble. If I can have this baby as easily as a ewe, it will be wonderful," Jochebed says cheerfully.

Mahala's ability to make perfect loaves of bread brings her familiar comfort and joy in the moment. She spent the morning hours grinding the wheat into flour and preparing the dough to be patted into loaves. She looks at the smoldering coals in the fire pit. When the coals have turned to a powdery gray, they are just the right temperature. She places the loaves in the heavy pottery pot and puts them in the pit. Within a short time, the smell of cooking bread wafts into the air joining the pleasant aroma rising from many other courtyards.

"When one has a duty, it must be done well," She often says. Attention to her duty to serve and her unwavering faith in the promise of a better life have molded her into the solid pillar that helps sustain her family despite continuing sorrow and loss.

"Child, women are not sheep. Your contractions have barely begun. The pain will come later. But the pain is not the important part of giving birth. It must be suffered, but the experience of bringing a new person into the world is the greatest joy it brings. This is such a magical part of life." She smiles.

"It sounds like it is time to call for Shiphrah." Mahala gets up. "I think we will need her here soon. She will guide you through everything you need to do for a smooth birth."

"I will go and call her," says Sarah taking her wrap to protect herself from the sun.

Although Sarah has suffered much, she maintains a cheerful attitude despite losing two pregnancies. One child was stillborn early in the first years of her marriage; the other pregnancy was spontaneously aborted during her grief over her husband Asa's death. Asa died in an accident while working on an Egyptian temple construction project. He and ten of his fellow Israelites were lost when a massive brick wall fell on them killing them all.

After Asa's death, his family sent Sarah back to her paternal family because she was childless. No man will ask for her hand in marriage. Men consider a woman unable to produce children cursed by God. Even so, Sarah is following in the footsteps of her mother as she learns patience in the face of suffering.

Shortly after Sarah leaves to fetch the midwives, word spreads quickly around the village. Women began to gather in the courtyard eager to learn and discuss the progress of the birth. They wait patiently, passing the time with idle chat to see who arrives. For the women, each arrival is significant.

Sarah returns followed by Shiphrah and Puah, each carrying a specially designed, unfired mud brick used in birthing. These experienced midwives and their helpers regularly attend the births of the Israelite children. They have earned the trust of all women in the tribes. Adah, the teenage daughter of Shiphrah trails close behind carrying special herbs and other supplies wrapped in a linen cloth. The women open a path for them as they enter the courtyard. Shiphrah pauses and assumes a determined stance as she addresses the group with important instructions.

"Everyone must stay in this courtyard. Only the chosen few women will go in the house. Please keep as quiet as possible. We want this baby to come into a world of quiet and peace." Shiphrah's voice is calm with practiced confidence. She fully expects all visitors to comply with her orders.

Shiphrah is nearing middle age. Some gray is appearing in her hair, and wrinkles are starting to form slight creases around her eyes. She has worked with birthing women since her late teen years when her mother, who was also a midwife introduced her to the profession of midwifery.

Entering the house, she finds Jochebed pacing restlessly. Hogla is holding her hand and supporting her as she walks back and forth across the room. The contractions are much more intense now.

They pause as a contraction engulfs the soon-to-be young mother. Shiphrah waits for the contraction to subside and examines the progress. Satisfied that all is well, she goes to the rear courtyard to supervise the preparations of herbs to ease pain, cloths to wrap around the baby, and salt to rub on the infant.

A small narrow east window and a matching one on the north afford subdued light and ventilation in the small room. A light breeze comes in through the windows and flows out through an opening in the roof. The women are calm. It is important to allow the birth to happen in a relaxed atmosphere. They speak encouraging words in low whispers to help Jochebed stay focused on her task. She soon discards her linen tunic to concentrate on the intense work ahead.

Puah unwraps the bricks from the linen and places them carefully on the floor. She motions for Jochebed to step onto the bricks. The unbaked mud bricks enable the prospective mother to assume a deep squat which encourages the baby to descend into the birth canal.

"Sweetie, are you comfortable with the bricks supporting you?" Even though Puah is six years younger than Shiphrah, she moves with confidence when she is working with a young prospective mother.

Jochebed squats as directed. "I think I can do it," she says, gasping for breath between pains. The perspiration is running down her face and spilling onto her shoulders. Her hands are wet as the contractions become more intense. She is struggling to stay on top of the pain.

As Hogla strokes Jochebed's brow, she says softly, "You can do this, my daughter. Your father dreamed last night that your sons are destined to be the salvation of Israel. You will not fail. He is sure the Almighty will bless this birth. He knows the Almighty will not forsake you."

Mahala quietly slips to the outer court. Eager for any news, the women immediately gather to her to hear the report of the progress.

"Kohath dreamed the baby is a boy! Praise the Almighty! I will have a grandson. He is going to be our long-awaited great leader. This is a wonderful day!" Mahala throws her hands up dancing with joy trying not to shout. The women, cackling with excitement, congratulate her good fortune with laughter and energetic dancing.

Suddenly Abahail arrives at the gate. "I see I am the last to know what is going on in this village! The senior wife of the tribe leader is always the last to be told about anything! Hogla did not bother to say anything to me! No matter, I am a forgiving person," she says through narrowed lips. "I see I am just in time to hear the baby is a boy."

Turning toward Mahala, she smiles through closed teeth. "Mahala, dear, I am so happy for our good fortune. Another grandson is wonderful news. Look. I brought a gift." Abahail holds up a carved figure of a dwarf.

"Mahala looks at the gift with alarm. "It is an Egyptian amulet of the god Bes! It's... It's...uh. Very ugly. You must not give this thing to Amram's wife," she stammers as she crosses her arms across her chest.

The gift is a wooden image of a dwarf with a large head, a grotesque smile, and a protruding tongue. He dances on a lotus flower holding a tambourine to make noise to scare away the demons.

"Of course, Dear. It is supposed to be ugly because Bes is a fierce dwarf that is scary. The Egyptians say Bes protects children from all evil things. The amulet is placed on the brow of the woman in labor, and he gives his protection. This god is extremely popular among mothers because he has such powerful magic. We have not heard from the Almighty lately. Every bit of help we can get in this day and time is welcome. But I must go in the house and let Bes do his work. It will help the baby come safely." Abahail smiles again with closed teeth.

"No! You cannot go in. Shiphrah said no one will go in until she gives us leave!" Mahala says firmly.

"Dear, I am the wife of Jochebed's father. I will go in now. I want to offer my help." She starts toward the door.

Suddenly a loud sound of "Ahhh!" comes from inside the house. Mahala steps in front of the door blocking the entrance. "You will not disturb the birth. The baby has not yet come. You will stay in the courtyard with the rest of us!"

Seeing her resolve, Abahail says, "Very well, dear. I will wait here with you. We can go in together when the babe has arrived."

In the house the birth is imminent. "You are doing very well but the baby must come down some more. You must start to push him out." Purah is rubbing Jochebed's lower back.

Jochebed feels an overwhelming urge to push. Pushing down with significant effort, she feels the baby go down through the pelvic bones. After a short rest between the contractions, she exerts another forceful effort pushing with Sarah and Ana supporting her arms. The top of the baby's head crowns and its hair is visible. After another intense push she feels an opening and releases the child into its new world.

Shiphrah extends her hands to grasp the child's head. She gently guides the baby as it slides out and then checks to make sure the umbilical cord is not wrapped around the neck as she examines the newborn carefully.

"It is a girl! The baby is a girl!" she exclaims, holding the child up for all to see. "You have a beautiful girl! She is an exceptionally strong child. Hear her cry."

Sarah and Hogla help Jochebed to a mat. Exhausted, the new mother rests on her back.

"Is the baby really a girl?" she asks weakly. "I want to see her."

"Yes, not a doubt about it. Your baby is a girl. See for yourself." Shiphrah places the infant, with the umbilical cord still attached, on Jochebed's stomach. Slimy with birth fluid, the child stops crying and looks at her mother for the first time. The tiny bright eyes staring from the smallest little face seem to say, "Here I am! I have been waiting to meet you, Mother."

An unbreakable cord binds the mother's heart permanently to the child. A completely new being has entered the world from her body. A new soul has come from her soul and magically entered the world. This little being is so much a part of her yet she is a unique individual. Suddenly everything in the world disappears into a blur. Gone is the intense pain and struggle of childbirth. This child is all that matters. Her baby smell, the special sound of her cry and the intense look in her bright eyes are memories that are forever implanted in the young mother's brain.

Tenderly Jochebed strokes the fragile, silken cheek. A fierce protective urge, like nothing she has ever experienced, washes over her. With Hogla's help, she sits up, takes the baby in her arms, and lifts her to her breast. As she feels the tiny, wet body against her bare skin, her heart jumps. "My precious, sweet little daughter, you are a magical experience too wonderful to describe." She whispers kissing the soft forehead. "I will call you Miriam."

Chapter 3:
The Priest, The Pharaoh, and their Plot

I became the becoming became, I have become the form of Khepri who came into being on the First Time...when I became, the transformations became, all the metamorphoses coming to pass after I had become." On Khepri from an Egyptian tomb.

Small flames from torches set in niches carved into the wall illuminate the small temple room. Light bounces off the shining scalps of the priests. A heavy odor of incense hangs in the stuffy air. Amenwau is wearing a leopard skin to signify his position as high priest to the Pharaoh. His six attendant priests are dressed in white linen robes with golden collars that glow in the torchlight. Ghostly shadows appear against the walls as the priests prepare for the Pharaoh's sacred rites.

To purify themselves for participation in these sacred rituals, the priests bathe their bodies, shave all their hair, and slather their bodies with scented oil in accordance with these most holy rites.

Amulets of jade carved in the shape of the scarab beetle swing from their belts. The beetle called Khepri symbolizes the eternal creations of their god who they believe brought about life. As the scarab beetle's larvae are buried in the earth and rise as a flying beetle, the Egyptian belief is that Pharaoh descends into the underworld at night. He battles demons and rises again victorious in the morning. The beetle symbolizes the divine Pharaoh, son of Re the sun god.

The priests are methodical in their tasks. All the sacred objects and utensils are meticulously cleansed as well. Everything is clean and polished. Their preparations for the ritual sacrifice must be perfect.

When the utensils are ready, they take standards with golden emblems of the all-seeing Horus, the hawk that represents the omnipresent, divine Pharaoh. They must adorn the holy image of their king and lord of the earth.

Amenwau carries an incense burner and a bronze bucket filled with water from the sacred temple lake. He sprinkles the purified water as the priestly procession moves toward a door sealed shut with a clay seal. The attendants wait while Amenwau alone approaches the door since only the high priest may enter this holiest place.

"I am the pure one; I alone can break the seal." He breaks the clay seal and opens the door to reveal a golden shrine of the ancient sun god veiled in fine linen and surrounded by sacred objects. As he carefully adorns the golden image, he chants in his full bass voice.

"Khepri, creates himself from nothing, He appears on the horizon above the mountains to bless men with his warming rays. His golden orb travels across the sky. He becomes RA, the supreme god of gods who at his zenith pours life-giving light upon the earth. At eventide, he is Atuj who disappears beneath the earth to battle the demons of the underworld. He is reborn again in the morning. Praise to our great god of all gods and lord of all lords. He will be reborn forever."

Completing the ritual, Amenwau sweeps his footprints from the dust on the floor to remove all traces of his presence. He prepares to go to the Great House of the Pharaoh, King of Egypt. Twice each year priests go to the palace when the sun's appearing is precisely right to perform the sacred rites for the Pharaoh.

Pink light illuminates the eastern sky when the priests arrive at the magnificent palace in perfect time with the sun's appearing. They cautiously approach the burly palace guards who regard them carefully. Peering closely at each man to determine his identity, guards acknowledge their presence with a slight nod before giving them leave to enter. Passing guards at every station, they finally arrive at the king's chamber door. The king's attendant calls to someone inside the chamber, receives an answer, and opens the massively heavy door slightly.

As elk might enter a meadow, the men approach with caution. Their senses are tuned to detect any hint of danger. Carefully they assess the air for different smells. Eyes scan for objects moved or different individuals present, and ears listen for every subtle sound before committing themselves to the king's specially designed chamber because any mistake could be fatal.

In a brief glance, the priests scan the room in minute detail. Amenwau senses a slight warning that something may not be as usual, but he cannot detect it for certain. The priests, keeping their eyes lowered, enter the room and fall to the floor to honor the king.

They repeat in unison, "King of kings, our lord of lords we welcome the light. May you be reborn forever and ever."

Pharaoh stands, arms lifted high, in front of a tall east window. The sun peeks above the distant horizon. The first shafts of light illuminate the figure. Rays from the rising sun bless the Pharaoh as he stands in front of the window.

Pharaoh chants, "Khepri creates himself from nothing. He is born again to rule the earth and sky. I am the son of Re. I bring light to the kingdom. All men, beasts and gods fall to worship me."

When the brilliant rays strike the golden collar, it blazes with dazzling light, illuminating Pharaoh's figure with startling brilliance. Pharaoh remains motionless for a time until the sun's light fully bathes the room with light.

The priests chant, "Oh, Khepri, great god, you create yourself to light the earth. We praise your wonderful greatness."

When the sun has risen past the window, the priests present the sacred objects to the king and anoint him with sacred oil. They help him to dress in a fine white linen tunic. The golden collar and all other jewelry that designate him as supreme Pharaoh complete his attire.

The ceremony concludes when Pharaoh dons his crown featuring a cobra positioned to strike. He sits in an elaborately painted chair. Like all objects dedicated to the king, images of the innumerable gods decorate the chair. The hawk god, Horus, is prominent. The all-seeing eye of the Hawk represents the all-seeing king who knows and governs all who are his subjects.

A servant, dressed in a traditional loincloth, brings a small box containing the ankh. A cross with a loop at the top forms the ankh which signifies to the Egyptians the power of life and death. The one who wields the power to control the ankh has the power of life and death over all lesser mortals. The king grabs the ankh from the box and settles in his chair.

He waves the ankh toward the priests who are nervously waiting for further orders. "Go now, all except the high priest."

Then pointing toward Amenwau, "You. Stay here!" he barks.

Amenwau waits, his palms sweating. He twists the amulet chain on his neck. While the others exit, he shifts his weight from one foot to the other. Beads of sweat form on his bald head. The guards move closer to the king. Pharaoh's chief of staff enters and stands close to the king. Amenwau stares at the floor, stiffening his legs to control their shaking.

A slight movement on the floor catches his eye. A lizard is slithering slowly along. Its color blends perfectly with the stone tiles. The reptile stops and remains perfectly still. Not even an eye is moving. A buzzing fly moves on its hair-thin legs toward the waiting lizard. Faster than a speeding arrow, the lizard's tongue hits with deadly accuracy. The fly disappears into the lizard's mouth. The space occupied by the fly is vacant as if the fly never existed. The triumphant lizard disappears into a crack between the stones in the wall. Amenwau's attention turns away from this little drama when Pharaoh speaks.

The Pharaoh asks abruptly, "How long have you been a high priest?"

"My Lord," answers Amenwau, fidgeting under the pressure of six pairs of staring eyes, "My father faithfully served the Pharaoh gods for more than twenty years. I served the previous Pharaoh for ten years. When Your Highness became Pharaoh, I continued worshipping faithfully as before."

"You oversee the scribes. Is this true?" demands the king.

"Yes, Your Lordship." The priest swallows hard as he prepares himself for a barrage of questions.

"Your father was a high priest before the revolution? Is this true?"

"Yes. Pharaoh."

"Then you should know all Egypt's history. You know about all the great Pharaohs and their deeds. Do you know about the revolution and the changes that came about when it happened? You have all the records of these things?"

"Yes. Pharaoh".

"I find no record about the Hebrews. What about these Hebrew shepherds? What did your father say about them? How did they come to Egypt? What gods do they worship? Tell me all you know about them."

Amenwau shifts his eyes upward and to the left, attempting to collect his thoughts. "They came from the land of Canaan to Egypt about 400 years ago when there was a severe famine over the entire world. Only Egypt had food to sell."

The king interrupts, "Egypt is the only place where enough grain can be grown and stored to feed large numbers of people in times of drought. Traders from all nations come every day to buy food here. They return to their country. Why did these people stay in Egypt? How did such low-class people get to stay on the best land in Egypt? Common Egyptians do not own land. How did these stinking shepherds get to stay on the best grazing land in all of Egypt?" The Pharaoh bellows.

"Because a Hebrew slave was able to predict the great famine Egypt was saved from ruin." The priest realizes his mistake too late.

"What?? What are you saying? What nonsense are you going to tell me?" the king yells.

"Tell me how could a Hebrew slave save Egypt? Impossible! A slave saved Egypt! Ridiculous! If you are going to tell me such lies, I can have your head now!" he shouts, waving the ankh toward the priest.

Amenwau remembers the unsuspecting fly. He thinks more carefully before speaking.

"Of course, it is impossible and ridiculous, my Pharaoh, I meant to say these people believe that one of their numbers who was a slave, saved Egypt. This is what they believe. Forgive my foolishness for not saying it correctly. These Hebrews came to Egypt to buy food because the wise Pharaoh stored enough food to feed many thousands of people. Egypt became rich despite the terrible famine." Amenwau steals a glance toward the king.

Pounding the chair arm with his fist, the king roars a question, "Why would this Pharaoh grant favor to these stinking, sheep-herding people? Tell me that!"

Amenwau's eyes look upward. Then he slowly starts his story again. "Pharaoh had a dream. The gods were giving him a message in this dream. He had to do everything possible to determine the meaning of the dream. None of Pharaoh's wise men could tell its meaning."

Amenwau steals another glance toward the king. The king is leaning forward. The black rings painted around his eyes intensify his expression of anticipation. Intent on every word as if each sentence is of extreme importance, he grips the arms of his chair. The white linen tunic enhances the dark contrast of his painted eyes. His beard is wrapped with a golden cord that shapes it into a cone that curls on the end.

Pulling himself up taller Amenwau raises his eyes the smallest bit as he takes a deep breath and continues, "One of the Pharaoh's attendants told the Pharaoh about a Hebrew slave who could interpret dreams. The slave was in a prison. Pharaoh, can you imagine people who would sell their young brother into slavery? That is exactly what these Hebrews did. These people sold their own young brother to a noble Egyptian. The Egyptian liked the young man. He even gave the slave control over all his wealth. But the slave was not content with the master's goods, he wanted the master's wife as well. When the slave was caught trying to take the good wife, the husband him to prison."

The king slams his fist on the arm of the chair. "That was too lenient a punishment! A slave should have been executed! Why wasn't he executed?" He looks at his attendants around him. They nod in agreement.

"No matter! Not all Pharaohs are smart. Go on!" The king waves his hand toward Amenwau.

"Yes, Your Lordship. These Hebrews cannot be trusted. They must not be treated with leniency."

Pausing briefly to study the king's expression from the corner of his lowered eyes, Amenwau continues his story.

"While in prison, the slave would interpret the meaning of dreams for his fellow prisoners. Pharaoh's trusted wine server who displeased his Pharaoh dreamed that he would be restored to the Pharaoh's favor. It came true just as the slave said. A baker, who displeased his Pharaoh dreamed…"

"Go on with your story about Pharaoh," snaps the king. "I don't want to know what the prisoners were dreaming."

The priest breathes deeply and sighs, "Yes, Pharaoh. As I was saying, the honorable Pharaoh determined to know the meaning of the dream. He was willing to do everything possible to know the message contained in the dream. When the king's wine server, who had been in prison with the Hebrew, told the king about the young man who could interpret dreams, the king sent for the slave." The priest shifts his weight and clenches his fists. He thinks deeply before continuing.

"I want to hear all this story. You can relax now."

Amenwau relaxes his legs and shakes his hands as he blows a puff of air through his lips.

"Thank you. You are kind. This Pharaoh knew a genuine wise man could tell the meaning of the king's dream. The Pharaoh knew the gods were giving him a message. He had to find out what the message was."

The priest steals a glance at the king again to see how the king is receiving his story.

"The dream concerned seven fat cows and seven skinny cows coming up out of the Great River. The skinny cows ate the fat cows. The skinny cows become no fatter after they had eaten the fat cows."

"What did the dream mean?" the king interrupts again.

"My Lord, the fat, sleek cows represented seven years of abundant grain crops. There would be an overabundance of grain harvested for seven years. But the good times would end. The skinny, ugly cows were seven years of poor crops. The bad years would be so bad they would eat up all the good years. The population would starve during the bad years unless preparations prevented it."

"Did the Pharaoh believe this slave?" asks the king skeptically.

"He did because the slave was the only man who knew the interpretation of the dream. He was the only man who could tell Pharaoh about the cows and the grain in the dream. All the king's wise men, even with their magic, could not tell Pharaoh the meaning of the dream." Amenwau holds his breath waiting for a response.

"How did the slave know about the dream? What magic did he have? How could he know more than all the wise men of Pharaoh's court?" the king demands to know.

"That impudent slave said the dream was a message from his god. This god has no name or image, yet the slave said the god told him the dream. The god told him to store grain during the good years and sell the grain when the bad years came. The Hebrews believe this slave, with the help of his god, saved Egypt from destruction."

"Do you believe this is true?" asks the king, as he twines his finger in the curl at the end of his beard.

"No, despite what the slave said, Pharaoh recognized Egypt's gods were talking to him in the dream. The Pharaoh wisely built great storage bins to store food during the good years to prepare for the bad years." The priest gestures with his hands to indicate the large size of the grain bins.

"The bad years were so bad the people traded their livestock, gold, and land for food. When the bad years were over Pharaoh owned all the livestock, goods, and land except what our priesthood owned. The Pharaoh was even richer and more prosperous than before the famine. That is the reason the Pharaohs own all land in Egypt today except for the land owned by our priesthood." Amenwau waits for the king's response.

"But why did the Pharaoh allow the Hebrews to settle in the best land in Egypt?!" the king roars.

Amenwau thinks carefully before he speaks, "This Pharaoh was not only wise, but he was also a man of his word. He made a vow promising a great reward to anyone, even a slave, who could tell him the meaning of his dream. He made the slave a ruler over all of Egypt. The king allowed the slave to settle his family on the best grazing land, but at that time there were only a few of these Hebrews. Since they were excellent cattle breeders, they tended the cattle for the Pharaoh."

The king waves the ankh toward the priest.

"Why are there no records in the tombs, in the records of kings, or on the temple walls? What was this slave's name? I have never heard anything about him. It does not seem plausible that a Pharaoh would give all this to detestable people. Are you sure this is accurate?"

"Your Lordship," the priest answers slowly, "after the revolution, the enemies of that Pharaoh erased all the records of him. This Pharaoh and the story of the slave were erased from the temple records. A new Pharaoh took his tomb. The slave's name was Zaphenath Paneah. The shepherds hold him in great honor. They call him Joseph."

A deep breath escapes from Amenwau before he continues, "Even though the slave was the vizier of Egypt, he had no tomb because he directed his family to preserve his bones and take them back to Canaan when they leave Egypt."

Startled, Pharaoh draws back suddenly. "When they leave Egypt! How are they going to leave Egypt? This is their idle dreaming! I will never let them leave!" he snorts, pounding his fist on the arm of his chair.

"Your Majesty, when the slave's family came to Egypt generations ago, there were only seventy men, but now there are more of them than stars in the sky! They are increasing faster than goats! This continuous multiplying must be stopped soon, or they will take over all of Egypt! These people will ruin our land!" Amenwau says emphatically waving hands.

"How do you figure? As you said yourself, they are excellent livestock breeders. They provide many cattle and a lot of produce through heavy taxes. Since they were conscripted into a labor force, they have accomplished many building projects. They are strong and can work hard. If one is lost while working, it is better than losing our own people. To lose a Hebrew is a small loss. They are quickly replaced. The more hands to do that work, the more the work gets done. This is good for the country and its economy. Besides, I want my tomb finished soon. The Israelites must support the skilled laborers. There must be no decrease in the labor force until my tomb is finished."

"Yes, your Lordship. Your word is law." The priest presses his lips tightly together.

Wrinkles knit Pharaoh's brow as he strokes his chin with his left hand. "You do not agree? Speak. What is the priesthood saying about these people?"

Amenwau clasps his hands in a prayer gesture. "I ask your ears to hear me carefully. These shepherds are filling our land so fast they will soon outnumber us. When there are more Hebrews than Egyptians, they will overpower their taskmasters and rise in rebellion. Some confirmed reports say the kings of Canaan are making alliances with their neighbors. They are talking about war against Egypt. What if the Canaanites decide to attack us? The Hebrews may rebel against us and join them. They believe the land of Canaan belongs to them. They believe their god promised to give Canaan to them. What would keep the Hebrews from secretly joining a pact with the Canaanites in exchange for land in Canaan?"

"That is a possibility we have been considering," the Pharaoh mutters under his breath.

The priest takes up his discourse again. "As I said, the Israelites possess the bones of the slave who was vizier of Egypt. He told his family to take the bones back to Canaan and bury them at the family burial site. This is proof the Hebs believe they will leave Egypt with a great victory. How can they do this without help from Canaan or other nations? Something must be done soon to stop the population explosion. We will be in very real danger unless there are tighter controls on them as soon as possible."

The king sits very still while continuing to stroke his chin for a long moment. "How would you control their population? I need slaves to do my building. What are your ideas? Do you have any ideas?"

Very much relieved, the priest says, "The priesthood has been considering several options. Would it please your Gracious Lord if I came back to present a plan to control the Hebrew population and make them more subject to your control? Will you give our plans thought?"

"I will hear your plan, but I do not want the working slave population to decrease until my current projects are completed. Go now! We are done here!" The king waves toward the door.

As soon as the priest has gone, the king turns to his chief of staff, "Get a message to General Ankerkhua. His army is camped on the southern border. In six months, his campaign should end. He will be back before the river rises. I need to keep the military informed of any important developments in this Hebrew crisis. If there is a major change of policy, the military must be here to keep the peace!"

Chapter 4:
The Dreadful Proposition

"Follow your desire, allow the heart to forget... Dress yourself in garments of fine linen... Increase your beauty, and let not your heart languish. Follow your desire and what is good. Conduct yourself on earth after the dictates of your heart" ......
An Ancient Egyptian song.

Shiphrah hurries to see who is banging loudly on her gate. An Egyptian court official stands waiting in a chariot as his assistant continues to knock. Suddenly apprehensive, she bids her children to stay out of sight. Quickly she hurries across the courtyard and cautiously approaches the gate.

"Are you Shiphrah, head of the guild of the Hebrew midwives?" the man demands to know.

"Yes, I am Shiphrah. I assist Hebrew women with childbirth." From behind the gate, she answers quietly as her apprehension grows. The horse, tossing its head, stamps its foot and blows loudly through its nostrils. The sweaty beast makes her more nervous.

"Come out here," the Egyptian commands.

Cautiously, Shiphrah opens the gate and steps out still holding onto the gate behind her.

"The Supreme Pharaoh of Egypt commands you to appear at the palace immediately."

Shocked, Shiphrah stammers, "What does his Supremacy, want from me?" Her heart thumps loudly in her chest.

"Do not question the Pharaoh! the official says, 'Come!' You must come now! Be at the palace courtyard as soon as possible. You will be told the Pharaoh's commands. The official slaps the reins on the horse's rump. With a snort, the horse starts off as the messenger jumps into the chariot.

"Why are you going to see the Pharaoh?" Dedan, Shiphrah's five-year-old son asks.

"I do not know. But you must stay here with Grandma and Adah. I will come back soon."

Dedan whines as he grabs his mother's leg. "The Pharaoh does not like us. What if you do not come back? What will we do?"

"I will come back. Do not say such silly things. You must do your duty and be very good to Grandma. Mind Ophir, too. She will take care of you." She stoops to hug him and comfort him.

Wrapping a linen shawl around her head and shoulders she leaves to begin the six-mile walk to the palace. Ahead she sees Puah.

"Puah! Puah! Wait."

Puah stops and waits for her to catch up.

"Did that man come to your house too?" Shiphrah says out of breath from running.

Stopping to wait for Shiphrah, Puah says, "Yes, he did. He was very scary. I do not like this at all. I know it cannot be anything good. Nothing the Egyptians ask of us is good for us. They always want us to give them something."

Puah's eyes dart left and then right. "What do they want? What can we do for them? All we do is help women give birth. How will that help Egyptian men? I have an awfully bad feeling about this."

Shiphrah agrees, "You are right Puah. We always must give up something important, but what can this mean? We must not ask them too many questions. It will only make them angry. We must be as cooperative as we can be."

When they arrive at the palace, guards allow them to enter the courtyard. A low stone bench in the corner provides a place to wait for further instructions.

Far above them, Nephre, Queen of Egypt, is looking down from her apartment window. This clear view of the front courtyard enables her to see all who enter or leave the palace via the main gate. Few visitors can escape her notice. Hebrew women are very rarely allowed onto palace ground.

The queen holds a mirror with a golden handle. Her large, thick black wig waits on her dressing table for her makeup to be applied before it will complete her wardrobe.

Nephre was selected as the wife of Pharaoh initially because of her elegant beauty and charm. Her elevation to favorite wife came when she beguiled her king with her flare for the dramatic. She learned quickly after her ascent to the position as premier wife of Pharaoh, if she wanted to retain her position, she must be aware of all that is taking place in the palace. She intends to make sure nothing catches her by surprise.

"Why are Hebrew women at our gate?" the queen asks as Titi, her lady-in-waiting, comes into the Queen's private quarters carrying makeup and toiletries. "They look as if they are waiting to enter the palace. Who are they? They would not come without an order from the Pharaoh. Only the king can grant permission to call Hebrews. Why would the king call Hebrew women? Pharaoh says Hebrews are detestable. This is strange."

"I do not know, my Queen. It seems very strange," the pretty young woman answers, as she places the tray of face paint and rare facial oils on a small, elaborately carved table. She proceeds to help her queen put on makeup. The final touch is done with a hair eyelash brush. Titi dips the brush into the jar of kohl and deftly paints wide black wings on the queen's eyelids. Then she gathers a black wig of long hair and positions it on the queen's head.

Titi is an unusually attractive girl who easily gets the attention of men. Nephre chose her to serve as one of her personal maids specifically because she has a talent for manipulating information from men. The girl is considered one of her most valuable resources for obtaining vital information concerning what is occurring in the palace.

Turning to face Titi, the Queen gives her a knowing look. "Then find out! 'I don't know' is never a satisfactory answer." Her bracelets make the familiar jingle that punctuates her order as Nephre waves toward the door.

"Yes, My Queen."

From a pottery jar hidden in a niche in the wall, Titi takes some silver coins and stuffs them into her folded sash before exiting the room.

Descending the long stone stairs, she goes to the palace ground floor. There she follows a dark corridor to the servant's quarters. When she approaches a heavy, wooden door with a small peephole, she raps three knocks, then two, then one sharp knock. An eye appears at the hole. Titi holds up the silver coins. When the door opens, she pushes the silver coins in the extended hand.

In a dirty room that smells of dirt and sweat, she is left alone where tunics, sandals, and other clothing worn by the slaves who work in Pharaoh's gardens are hanging. Titi selects one of the garments which she pulls over her dress. Rough crude sandals are exchanged for her soft shoes. A worn, long neck wrap is arranged over her head and pulled low down below her eyebrows, then wrapped around her neck so that it covers her chin and mouth.

Grabbing a basket, she goes to the vegetable storage bins in the adjacent room. There she fills the basket with onions. Carrying the basket, she heads for the main piazza at the palace entrance.

As she nears the open courtyard where guards are always on duty, she surveys the scene. A gigantic image of Isis watches over the merchants, palace workers, and slaves who are intently going about their daily business of keeping Pharaoh's Great House running smoothly.

Far across the courtyard, Titi spots Puah and Shiphrah sitting huddled together on a stone bench as far out of the way of the busy traffic as they can manage. Two palace guards are standing beneath the image of Isis in deep conversation. One of them motions toward the midwives.

Titi assumes the slow, shuffling gait of a slave who was taken from a conquered nation by Pharaoh's soldiers. She weaves her way through the crowd toward the guards. First, she dodges a cart filled with melons that are being pulled by a goat, and then she pulls away from a rude fellow who tries to take one of her onions.

When she is within earshot of the guard's conversation, she appears to stub her sandal against a stone on the tiled pavement. The basket tips. Three onions fall to the pavement. Stooping to retrieve the straying onions, she puts the basket on the floor and remains squatting, pretending to be adjusting her sandal straps. Her particularly keen ears catch bits of the conversation before the guards walk away.

Titi takes her basket and returns to the servants' quarters to rid herself of the dirty tunic and report to the Queen. Coming into the Queen's chamber, she finds the queen still watching from her window as she preens in front of a mirror.

"Are those wrinkles forming around my eyes? I thought that balm was going to keep them away! Do you know which merchant sold this balm, Titi?"

"No. I did not go to buy the balm, my Queen. But I did find some information on the Hebrew women who are in the courtyard."

"Wonderful!" The Queen smiles, "You are so skilled in getting information! Tell me now. Who are they?"

"These women are Hebrew midwives That means they deliver babies," she announces proudly. "Is Your Highness pleased I was able to find out so quickly?"

"Midwives? Midwives! How do you know they are midwives?" The queen puts the mirror down on the table and throws her hands high in the air before bringing them to either side of her head. The many bracelets on her arms clatter noisily.

"Why on earth are midwives here? What can they know about delivering babies that our people do not know? I must know what is going on. This looks suspicious. When did the king get into the business of delivering babies? I will not leave this room until I know what is going on!"

Titi says, "Your Highness, I do not know why they have come. I know they are midwives because I overheard one of the guards say the king called the midwives to come at once. I did not hear the rest of the conversation. He did not say why the king called them."

"Titi, you know I do not like being kept in the dark! They always try to keep me in the dark. I will not have it. Use your skill once more! Go now and find out why those women wait at our gate." The queen waves forcefully, pointing to the door. This time the jangle of the bracelets gets louder making their clattering music.

Wearing her most colorful dress and extra makeup, Titi returns to the main palace entrance where she finds the guard whose conversation she overheard standing at his post beneath the image of Isis.

"Hi, Garai," she purrs as she approaches him. "How is your day going? It looks like the piazza is extra busy today."

Garai looks at her suspiciously then a slight smile appears in his eyes. "You do not come here often. I have not seen you around in a while. Why are you here today?"

"I had a few minutes and needed a break to get some air. It is a nice day. It feels good to get out in the air." She draws in a breath of air and lets it out with a satisfied smile. Then she looks all around the quadrangle toward every corner of the space. Her eyes rest on the stone bench where the midwives are waiting.

"Who are those Hebrew women sitting on that bench? Why would Hebrew women be here? They look like they may be midwives. Why would Hebrew midwives be called to the palace?"

Sweat beads appear on Garai's brow. His knuckles turn white as he grips hard on his spear. His left hand goes to his neck. He twists the cord that holds the jade amulet he wears as protection from evil spirits.

"How do you know they are midwives? Do they look different from other Hebrew women?"

"All I know is the queen asked me to find out why midwives are in the piazza. Someone must have secretly told her about the midwives, but they did not tell her why they were here."

Titi raises her eyes upward as she throws up her palms in a clueless gesture. "The Queen told me to find out why these women are here. She will be incredibly happy if I bring her the information. She even said I can take this evening off when the guard watch changes."

Titi gives him a playful glance, her eyelashes flutter, and a sly smile twists her mouth. The cone of scented wax she wears in her hair melts with her body heat allowing the sweet musky scent of the perfume to fill the air.

Squirming, the guard stares at her for a moment, caught in the dilemma of the coveted invitation and his duty to his king. The intoxicating sensual scent of the wax fills his nostrils. He shuffles his feet, his head spins, and his judgment flies away.

His mouth opens in a twisted smile. "Wait here. Don't leave." Garai strides across the piazza to the station where his fellow guard Cepos, keeps his watch. Garai looks back to make sure Titi is still waiting at the statue of Isis where he left her.

"Hey, man, can you help me?" he asks as he nears Cepos.

"What's up?" Cepos says, looking toward him.

Garai points with his thumb at Titi who is waiting on the far side of the courtyard.

"Oh, yeah!" Cepos grins, "She's a hot one! Looks like you got lucky for tonight. But you better handle this one like a basket full of cobras if you want to see your twentieth birthday celebration! What is she asking?"

"Uh," Garai stammers, "The Queen wants to know why those midwives are here at the palace." Garai feels his neck prickle like small pins are pricking him. The blood drains from his face.

"How do I handle this?" he gasps.

Cepos says seriously, "Man, you don't want to pass up an opportunity like this. But you better not tell her the truth. That could get you to your grave early. Tell her something to convince her you know what you are talking about, but make sure it is something you can safely deny if you need to. Oh, man! Why didn't she come over to my post?"

"Maybe she just thinks I am better looking" Garai savors his good fortune knowing Cepos is jealous. "If I don't tell her something convincing, she won't ask me anything else. What should I tell her that will not get me into trouble?"

"Why ask me?" Cepos shrugs. "If you don't learn to think fast, you won't be here very much longer anyway."

Garai scans the surrounding courtyard. His eyes move from the midwives to a group of African women who are gathered some yards from the Hebrews. He notices two of the Africans are obviously in the latter stages of pregnancy.

"Look at those black cows. Their little goblins will be dropping out soon!" Garai exclaims.

Cepos chuckles. "It would be funny to see those Hebs go into action if the Africans started to drop the little urchins right this minute!

Garai hits his fist on his hand triumphantly, "Wait! That's it. That's what I will tell her. The African slaves need the Hebrews' help in giving birth. Thanks man! Maybe you will be the lucky one next time! See you."

Garai turns on his heel and trots back to the statue of Isis where Titi waits.

When he comes close enough to Titi to smell the perfume again he says, "The midwives have come to instruct the African slaves about assisting their women in childbirth. The Africans are losing too many babies. Did you say you will be around tonight?"

Surprised, Titi muses, "The Hebrews must be very skilled in delivering babies if they instruct others in their craft."

"Oh. Yes! They know more about delivering babies than any women in all of Egypt. This is the reason Pharaoh has called them. You know we need the African slaves. How would all the work around this palace be done?" Garai studies her face intently to see if she believes his story.

"Oh! now I get it!" she says triumphantly. "The Hebrews are multiplying so fast because their midwives are so skilled. You are a sweetheart! The queen will be so happy with me! I will see you here later when you get off work, Garai," purrs Titi.

With a smile, she turns to leave, then blows a kiss to him before dashing away to tell the queen all she learned.

When Shiphrah and Puah are bidden to enter the palace, a tall handsome eunuch along with five beautifully dressed Egyptian court women greet them with great fanfare.

The eunuch has charge over the women's court. His primary duty is to look after the comforts of the wives and daughters of Pharaoh and see that the serving maids are attending to their duties.

"Ladies, welcome to Pharaoh's Great House. I am Fazel, servant of the Almighty Pharaoh, King of Egypt, at your service." He introduces himself with a graceful flourish of his hands as he bows toward them. "You are our honored guests. We will celebrate this wonderful occasion with a lovely party. But first, you must dress properly for the festivities." He claps his hands and smiles broadly showing white shining teeth which gleam against his dark face.

Three slave women with shining ebony skin come to his call. They are lithe and slender as gazelles. One is carrying a small, wooden, gold-inlaid chest. She opens the chest and reveals an assortment of gold jewelry. The second carries yards of beautiful cloth. The third has a flask of scented oil and three fans made of ostrich feathers. Fazel motions for the slave to bring the cloth near so Puah can touch it.

When Puah feels the royal purple waves of color, her rough, toil-worn fingers stroke the smooth, soft material. The cloth feels light and silky, unlike her coarsely woven tunic with its ragged hem, ash stains, and embedded dirt. She is keenly aware of her unpolished appearance in the presence of the Egyptians with their oiled bodies and beautifully-fashioned clothes.

"Ladies, you will not believe your eyes when you see what we will do for you. Please excuse me. I will leave while you dress." Fazel exits quickly.

A transformation begins. The lovely slaves bid Shiphrah and Puah to remove the dingy tunics. With scented oil rubbed on the skin, dust from the long dusty road disappears. The sweet, spicy scent of the oil replaces the odors of sweat and cooking smoke. Soft fabric slippers replace their rough, worn sandals.

Soon they are wearing beautiful dresses made with silky-smooth purple linen cloth that is draped over their bodies. It falls in brilliant cascades of color. A multi-colored sash tied around the waist completes the dress. A clasp of gold holds the drape in place at the shoulder. Golden necklaces and bracelets adorn their neck and arms. Their hair shines like the gleaming coat of a fine black horse when the slave women comb scented oil into it. Golden combs hold the elaborately styled hair in place. Finally, with sure quick strokes the slaves deftly paint eyeliner around the eyes. A little red ochre brushed on their cheeks completes the makeover. With a smile, one of the slaves holds an ivory-handled mirror to Puah.

For a long minute, she stares at the image looking back at her. "Who is this?" she asks. It is difficult for her to comprehend her transformation. The midwives stare at each other in disbelief. The humble women with ragged clothes, tangled hair, and dirty feet have changed into fashionable women of the king's court.

The Egyptian women surround the two incredulous midwives with exclamations of "Oh how pretty you are! You are ready for the grandest celebration."

"How lovely you look, my dears! Fazel exclaims, as he reappears from a side door and takes each by the arm to escort them to colorfully painted chairs. Two of the Nubians station themselves on either side of the table to stir the air with the ostrich fans.

"You are beautiful. You arouse the jealousy of Isis herself, the loveliest of all goddesses. You look divine! Imagine when this is your accustomed way of adorning yourselves, you will dine on wonderful food and wine." Fazel smiles broadly.

He signals with a clap of his hands. Young girls appear, each carrying a large tray piled high with luscious grapes, sweet cakes of varying shapes, roast duck, and gazelle seasoned with rosemary, and spice wine. They place a tray on the banquet table and the other on a separate table for the Egyptians, who consider eating with Hebrews degrading.

"Taste the goodness of your king's favor. Dine from the king's own table. Enjoy yourselves. Do not let tasty food wait." Fazel picks up a tidbit of spiced roasted duck. "Here, taste this luscious little goody. Your tongue will melt with delight." He places it in Puah's hand and then takes one for Shiphrah.

The Hebrew women timidly taste the food. Such treats are a radically new experience for those whose diet is primarily barley bread, fish, and vegetables. They enjoy meat usually for special festivals. The mouth practically explodes with delight after each bite. Never imagining how exciting food could taste, Puah reaches for another bite.

Fazel clasps his hands together and then places them on either side of his chin. "Your king, The Pharaoh, wants to be your friend. He knows you are skillful in bringing children into his kingdom. He knows how hard you work. Ladies, on this day your lives will change. You have gained the Pharaoh's favor. Let us enjoy His Lordship's graciousness. Aren't the king's goodies so wonderful? Isn't this fun? We have only begun to enjoy his Highness's bounty. See what else is waiting to delight you!" Fazel claps again.

Five women dancers dressed in gold jewelry and sheer linen breeches prance into the room accompanied by musicians. Soon the room is filled with the sounds of tambourines, flutes, and drums. Twirling, swirling, and waving brilliantly-colored banners to the beat of the music, the dancers fill the room with pulsating rhythm and billowing clouds of breath-taking color. As soon as one dance stops, more dancers appear. They perform routines with amazing acrobatics.

Puah stares completely transfixed. Sounds, tastes, smells, and sights transport her from her world of smoky cooking fires, sweaty demanding work, and blowing sand to a place of exotic, opulent luxury she never imagined.

When the last dance is finished, the trays are removed. Only Puah and Shiphrah remain sitting in the painted chairs. Fazel asks, "Did you enjoy this delightful show? Don't you wish you could enjoy such wonders every day?"

"This is nice," Shiphrah says, " but what can we, humble midwives do for a great king? Why would the king want to give us such wonderful things? I do not know why you are doing this for us. Please tell us what we are to do for His Great Highness.".

"I can certainly understand your confusion. There are very few people in this entire kingdom who gain such favor with His Lordship, the Almighty King. His Gracious Lordship, who holds the power of life and death for us all, does ask favors from you. Considering everything the king is willing to give you, it will be a small favor you must do in return." He smiles that wide-charming smile.

Shiphrah goes on, "All we know is working in the fields. Our only skill is helping women give birth. We do not know how to do many other things. What kind of favor does the King ask of us?"

Fazel ignores the question. "So, tell me, when you are helping women as they give birth, do any of the babies fail to make it into the land of the living?"

"Yes," says Shiphrah, wondering where this question is leading, "Sometimes a child is stillborn, or it does not take its first breath. If it is weak, it may die. There is nothing we can do about that. Why do you ask?"

Fazel says immediately, "Since children often die at birth this means the gods allow them to die. There is nothing anyone can do about that. Isn't that, right?"

"Yes, this is true," Shiphrah answers thoughtfully. "We are not gods. We only help mothers bring their children into the world safely. A safe birth most often depends on how healthy and strong the mother and child are."

"There! You said yourself, you cannot always save the children." Fazel declares flatly. "Many of the babies die. What if you cannot save many of them? No one can blame you. No one would really know whether you did your best or not."

Becoming very uneasy, Shiprah slowly requests, "I do not understand what you are saying. You are talking in riddles, please tell me so I can understand His Lordship's will."

"Alright, I will say it clearly. This is His Supreme Pharaoh's command. When you are assisting a birthing woman, check the sex of the child. If it is a male, kill it. Pretend it died in the birth process. But you must not let any male child live. If the child is a female, you are to save her. You must tell this to all your midwife helpers. Do you understand Pharaoh's commands?" Fazel says smoothly as if he is giving instructions on preparing a dinner.

Stunned and feeling the blood drain from her face, Shiphrah says weakly, trying to grasp the horror of the message, "Are you saying we are to kill Hebrew sons? How can the king ask us to do such a terrible thing?"

"Let us not think of it as killing, let us just say it is a step to a better life for you and your families. Very few Egyptians will be granted this kind of opportunity. For Hebrews, it is almost unknown. Thousands of people would beg for this opportunity. Think how honored you are. The Pharaoh has personally called you to his Great House. He is offering you a great reward for your services."

"What if we do not want to do this?" Puah hesitates. "I have never deliberately hurt a child in my life. I am not sure I can intentionally hurt a baby. I certainly don't want to…" Her voice trails away.

"There, there–no one really wants to harm a baby, but you will not think much about it in time because everyone must obey the king's command if they want to live. If you do as you are commanded, you will live richly. If you do not, you will watch your children die a death so terrible even battle-hardened soldiers beg for mercy. Then you and the rest of your family will die the death as well. But there is no need to talk about that. You will do as His Lordship commands. Any other decision is very, very foolish. This is the end of the question. There is no other way, my dears. I will check on your progress in time. We will have another party when you have made good progress. You may keep the gold jewelry as a down payment for your services, but you must go now. We will celebrate with even more fun next time." Fazel waves them off and exits the room. The party is over.

Shiphrah and Puah remove the fine clothing. As they don their worn tunics, they remember the world where they belong. Shiphrah stares at the pile of gold jewelry. "Should we take this?" she asks Puah.

"If we do not take it, they will think we do not want to obey Pharaoh's commands. We will be in more trouble," Puah says.

Shiphrah picks up the jewelry and wraps it in Puah's scarf. They take their leave of the palace to begin the long painful journey back to their home.

Long shadows of the buildings are starting to creep across their path as they depart the city. Trudging slowly homeward, they are silent until they see the village in the distance. Puah breaks the silence.

"Do you really believe we will not think about it after a while? I cannot stop thinking about it. Possibly, it is just a step to save our families and our own lives as well. The clothes were so lovely! The food was so good! If the Pharaoh orders it, there is nothing we can do. There is no other way for us to stay alive and save our own children. I cannot even imagine watching my children die a terrible death. I never thought I could kill a baby. I do not know if I can do it. Will our helpers do it if we order it? What else can we do?" she sobs.

"I am thinking about my children, too, Puah. We may have no choice but to obey Pharaoh's orders. This could be the only way to save ourselves and our families." Shiphrah responds.

Her eyes have not left the dusty road during the entire walk. The crimson glow in the western sky is paling into a soft mauve. Twilight softly erases the shadows as they near the village. A few scattered stars are blinking in the overarching sky. The air is cooling. Sounds amplify in the crisp air. The low hoots of an owl echo in the distance. A cow moos, calling her calf. Joyful shouts of children chasing each other, carefree and happy, reach their ears. A mother calls her young ones in. Others shout happily, enjoying those last minutes of play before retiring for the night. The sounds are familiar and comforting.

Shiphrah stops and listens. "Do you hear them, Puah? Hear their happy voices. Without these children, the village would be as dead as these stones."

She kicks rocks on the path. "We helped these little children enter the world. We heard their mothers moan in pain. We saw the wonder on every mother's face as we placed the newborn baby in her arms. When a mother sees her child for the first time is one of the most beautiful moments a woman can experience. We are there to help her know that joy. When a woman has endured so much pain, to experience such joy, will we turn her joy to despair by taking her child from her? Will we drain the life out of our women by taking their children? Can death be more terrible than this? Will beautiful clothes, tasty food, and rich wine be worth the betrayal of our people? Can we ever look in the face of a mother whose child we have killed? Are we cruel monsters like the Egyptians who do not care if our people suffer?"

Puah is silent for a moment. "Oh, Shiphrah! You are right as usual. I do not want to hurt any child. I really do not. I am just so scared! So horribly scared! I do not want to see my children die. What can we do? Pharaoh knows everything. He will surely know if we do not do what he is commanding us. They keep records of every birth. What can we do?" Wringing her hands, she wails," Please, please. Tell me what we can do!"

Shiphrah crosses her arms across her chest and pulls her tunic close around her body. She looks up into the night sky as if searching for an answer. More blinking stars are decorating the measureless deep blue expanse.

"I do not know. At this moment I do not know what we can do. Somehow there just must be a way out of this. Surely there is a way to save ourselves and the lives of all the children. We will search until we find it."

Chapter 5:
Doubt and Fear

"Praise to thee, O Nile, that issues from the earth and cometh to nourish Egypt, Thou art verdant, O Nile, thou art verdant. He that makes man to live on his cattle, and his cattle on the meadow." An Egyptian song

"Remember this, Son. When you see Khepri, the scarab beetle, appear on the mud you will know the river is starting to rise. Our god, Khepri, brings renewal and rebirth. You know this is true because the river brings fresh water and black soil from far away mountains. Nearly every year we get water and fertile soil that grows good crops. We do not suffer drought and famine as other nations. Our gods are good to us. They give us all good things." Mut points toward the baskets of clothing stacked near the river's edge.

Punt, his seventeen-year-old son, takes a garment from the basket and wades over to his father who stands knee-deep in the water. Mut's short, bowed legs tense as he plants his feet firmly in the mud to prevent losing his footing on the slick river bottom. After swishing the garment in the water and rubbing out the stains, he pulls the tunic around a post secured in the riverbed. Using a wooden stick, he twists the wet garment to wring out the water and then hands it to Punt who goes back to place it in the basket of clean, wet clothing.

Mut looks at the swirl of muddy water rising from the river bottom as his son drags his feet. "Pay attention. Pick up your feet. You are stirring up the mud. Do you think we can get these clothes clean in muddy water?"

Punt looks at the swirl of muddy water behind him, He shrugs his shoulders. Mut waits impatiently while the mud settles and Punt comes back with another garment, this time carefully placing his feet so he does not stir up the mud.

The boy listens idly as his father continues his discourse.

"Because of our divine Pharaoh, son of Re, and the gods of the river give us our life of prosperity. We enjoy a good life of peace and abundance. May the Pharaoh rule this land forever."

Punt wets the stained garments, places them on a rock and begins to beat the stains with a wooden paddle. He wets the fine linen again, rubs it roughly, and hands it to his father who swishes it in the water.

"Every day we enjoy the goodness of the gods. We know our station. If we continue to do our duty nothing will disturb us. See how beautiful this linen is I washed for Master!"

Mut holds up the shining, white linen tunic and then continues his discourse.

"It is our duty and pleasure to wash these beautiful clothes for the master's household. This is the duty assigned to us by our sacred fathers who served the Pharaoh. I wash clothes as my father washed. You will wash your clothes as well. It is a good duty. We are given bread, vegetables, beer, and meat during festivals. We can fish as much as we want. We have a house. What more do we need?" Mutt asks rhetorically, not expecting an answer from his son who appears not to be listening. Mutt continues his speech anyway.

"During the time of the last full moon, a camel trader who has traveled to many different countries told me our Egypt is very much richer than any other land. That proves it! Our gods are the most powerful and wisest of all the gods. Our gods are very good to us. We show our gratitude to the deities with our many festivals. How good it is to dance, sing, and offer our sacrifices to the gods! The festivals are the reward we get for our service. Pharaoh, son of Re, is a very hard god. Working in the heat deserves some pleasure. He allows us much pleasure."

"Oh yes!" says Punt suddenly interested.

"Oh! It's only a month until the Dog Star festival! I can't wait! I sure hope we get plenty of beer this time! Last year, old Pharaoh was feeling good. We had jars and jars of beer! I got so drunk I had to be dragged home every night," he giggles.

"When those girls dance naked at the festivals, I go wild. It makes me feel like a happy goat. I can dance like a rooster. Ohh! Weee! Weee!" He rolls his eyes. His face twists into a silly grin.

The boy leaps from the water onto the beach. With his fists in his armpits, he flaps his elbows up and down like the wings of a large fowl. Thrusting his chest out his skinny legs go up and down to mimic the strut of an amorous rooster. He sings a raucous, squawking song that includes some roosters' crows. The dance ends when he hops high in the air three times, making his hair fly up and settle around his head like a heap of charred straw.

"You are getting behind with your work. Get back here!" Mut orders.

Punt returns to the water to continue his work. He is excited to talk about the festival.

"Last year six of us guys were having a wild old time until we bumped into those stupid Hebs, Beker and Perez. Those idiots put on feather masks and started dancing crazy in front of everybody. They thought we wouldn't know them. Stupid sheep men! We knew them by their smell! When Perez stepped on my foot, I hit him in the nose. He was so plastered he fell flat and didn't know when we dragged him to a ditch and rolled him in. You should have seen him when he hit the cold water. He came out so fast! We laughed so hard my stomach hurt! Then we chased them home in a hurry. We will teach those sheep men to leave our women alone and stay away from our festivals!"

"Son, don't get too friendly with the Hebs. Those people have strange ideas. They are breeding as fast as goats. They are as strong as mules. Pharaoh has them building storage buildings for us. It is the least they can do since they have our grazing lands. Listen to your daddy. You just be careful. Don't get friendly with the Hebs."

Punt yells, "They hit on our women! They want to participate in our festivals! They even try to steal our gods! We will fix them! I heard Pharaoh had plans to control their numbers. That will serve them right! I hope Pharaoh kills all of them! We would be better off! The next time Beker and Perez and all the rest of their stinking sheepmen friends come to our festivals, they will wish they never saw the Nile River."

Looking up, Punt sees Jochebed, Sarah, Tirzah, Judith, and Ana coming down the path along the river's edge. Tirzah is seven months pregnant.

"Look! Here comes a herd of she-asses now. Oh! Wee! Look at that one!"

When the women come near, he bends his back to thrust out his belly and holds his arms out in front of his stomach to make a gesture like a pregnant woman's belly.

"Eeee Hawww! Eeee Hawww!" he screeches braying like a donkey.

Pulling aside his loincloth, he exposes his privates.

"Look at this! See what I have!"

While making copulating gestures with his hips he holds his fingers to his head to represent a donkey's ears as he cavorts around the women, braying ever louder.

Egyptians working on a boat at the river's edge look up and laugh as if it is all a clever joke. Making obscene gestures, they yell out cat calls and laugh.

The five women draw closer together in a tight group. They continue walking as if they do not see or hear the men shouting. Obscenities fill the air. The insults fall on them as dung splatters on their faces. Eyes to the ground, they walk as fast as they dare until they have gone beyond the range of Punt's interest.

Jochebed has never known anything but contempt from the Egyptians. She considers their cruelty a harsh reality of life to be endured along with the heavy taxes and forced labor. Until now she simply ignores the insults as just one more hardship heaped on her by a people who have no love or pity for her. A shudder passes through her body. Clutching her stone reed cutter under her tunic, she feels a growing anger coming from deep within. She wants desperately to do something to stop this cruelty. At present there is nothing she can do except endure it.

Reeds must be harvested for making essential baskets. The women trudge farther down the river to an isolated place where the reeds grow thick. When they come to their accustomed place, they scan the area for crocodiles. Slowly they wade into the shallow water. Each finds her place to work. The tough papyrus reeds are cut with stone knives until enough have been gathered to make a large bundle for each one to carry.

They wait and watch until most of the men working along the river have gone before they hoist the bundles onto their backs and slowly trudge back to the edge of the village.

The weaving shed located on the outer edge of the settlement, serves as a gathering place where women meet for weaving baskets. Its basic structure is a low wall constructed of mud bricks with cane poles set in the bricks. A framework of cane poles forms the basic foundation of a roof. Bundles of green reeds are placed on the cane pole structure. When the reeds are completely dry and ready to be used for weaving the baskets, they are replaced with newly-cut bundles of green reeds.

The women arrive at the weaving shed, taking the dry reeds off the shed roof and replacing them before settling into their basket-making.

In the corner of the shed are pottery jars with lids hold bone-weaving needles, stone cutters, and notched wooden spacers used in the construction of the skillfully-woven baskets. Cushions and blankets are stacked along the walls to provide comfortable sitting while working.

Propped on goat-hair cushions, they twist the dry reeds into tight strands which form the basic material for their spiral-designed baskets. The pile of twisted reeds grows large enough to provide each worker with enough to make her basket grow quickly.

When there is a lull in the small talk, Sarah changes the mood as she puts into words the thoughts everyone has been contemplating for days.

"Our God cares about faithful women and their children. 'There is nothing too hard for the Lord' is what my grandmother said when she told us about our ancient mother Sarah. Sarah was too old to have the promised child, but God allowed her to give birth. He did the impossible for her. Will our God do the impossible for all of us now? Surely if he can enable an old woman to have a child, he will save our children." Looking from one woman to the other Sarah seeks agreement and affirmation.

Ana began her basket by weaving a circular base with long regularly-spaced stems of reed radiating from its center. She drops the circular woven pinwheel into her lap as she uses her hands to punctuate her words.

"I want to believe these stories are true, but where is the Almighty now? I cannot see Him. How do I know He is here? The Egyptians have all kinds of images of their gods. We can see what they look like. Why can't we see the Almighty? Things are getting harder and harder, but we have not heard anything new about the Almighty lately. No one in our village is like our father, Abraham, who, we are told, talked personally with God in his visions. Sometimes I wonder if the stories really are true or just made up by people who want to keep us going because our lives are so hard. How can we know they are true?"

Jochebed responds, "I have wondered about this as well. My father is so sure about the Almighty God. He says God cares for us, but when I hear that Pharaoh wants to kill our children, I wonder if this God will see what is happening. Pharaoh constantly watches over our lives. Horus's eye sees all. There are some of our own people who want to gain favor from Pharaoh. They even report to the Egyptian scribes every time there is a birth. How do we tell the Almighty our children are in danger? Will He care? Will He help us?" She hacks at the excess unruly straws with her stone knife.

"Yes. I'm very worried about that too. This baby is due soon." Tirzah says, patting her expanded belly.

"I am praying this baby is a girl. I know Caleb wants a boy even though we already have Ezra, but I cannot face it if they take my baby. It is too horrible to imagine." Tears appear in her eyes. She shudders in terror. She has not started weaving since the conversation began.

Choking back tears, Tirzah says, "The midwives say they will not kill any babies even if Pharaoh orders them to do it. How can they refuse Pharaoh's orders? That is the reason I am so afraid. How can a woman refuse to do what a king tells her to do? He will kill them and their children if they try to refuse. It is terrible to think that the midwives who come to help us give birth may try to kill our baby. But it is not their fault. There is nothing they can do."

Jochebed says emphatically as she stabs at the unruly straws, "Puah and Shiphrah are brave women. They will not kill your baby. I would not kill a baby even if a king told me to do it. I would rather die than kill a baby. Besides, if they do kill even one baby, we will not call them to help us. We will have our children with no help from them!"

Judith snorts, "You would not be so sure of yourself if the king told you to do it. You already have a son, but if you do have another, you will have to give him up just like the rest of us."

Jochebed retorts but in a softer voice, "Maybe I am too sure of myself, but that is the way I feel right now. Shiphrah and Puah can be trusted. I am sure this is true. If not, we must find another way to have our children without their help. I am very glad Aaron is already passed one year old. Surely, he is safe. I hope I will not be expecting another child any time soon.

Sarah says, "This is one more trial we must face. We will have to be very watchful to see what is going to happen. We will keep our ears open to learn everything we can."

Angrily, Ana spits out her words, "We are forced to pay the Egyptians part of all our grain, as well as our baskets, linen cloth, and everything else we own! They demand that we make bricks for them! We cannot do anything about it. Now they want to kill our children! What can we do?

There is nothing any of us can do."

Sarah, looking at each of them, says, "I know well the bitterness of losing my children. I know the pain and anguish of losing my entire family. My family is no more. All have been taken away. It is an empty feeling. I try to understand it, but at times the sadness of loss is so overpowering that I cry and cry when no one is around."

Her eyes cloud with tears. "I trust someday Almighty God will restore my honor and take away my grief. My heart is with all the women who are worrying about the fate of their children. My heart is hurting for all of you."

The shadows are growing longer and darker; the cooling air signals the day of work is over. Putting away their tools and materials the women leave the conversation for another time.

Jochebed arrives home before twilight. Aaron, who is just learning to walk, strains against Miriam's hand as he joyfully squeals with delight at the sight of his mother. He wobbles toward Jochebed on unsure little legs. She lifts him in her arms.

"I see you are taking more steps today, Little One. Miriam is teaching you well. See what a good sister you have!" she says kissing him.

Mahala says eagerly, "There has been some excitement while you were away. Hannah, your cousin gave birth. She has a son! It is wonderful. The child is healthy and strong, but this child is a secret. No one except close family is to know about him. We must keep quiet about this. No one went to the house to greet the new baby. We only talked about it in whispers when only a very few trusted people were near."

"Were any midwives there? What did Shiphrah and Puah do? Did they try to kill him?" The young mother asks anxiously.

"No, Puah and Shiphrah sent secret messages from some trusted friends saying that no one should call the midwives unless they believe the mother or baby is in danger," Mahala explains. "Too much talk could get Puah and Shiphrah in trouble.

Little Miriam has been listening intently with wide eyes. "I will not tell anybody!" she declares.

"I don't like that old Pharaoh! I hope a snake bites him. I will not let him take my baby brother! I will kick him and punch him in the eye." She kicks and punches at the air as if fighting a phantom foe. Four-year-old Miriam is seldom lacking for words or opinions. She knows no strangers and happily chatters to anyone who will listen.

Jochebed, stroking Miriam's hair, lovingly affirms, "You are a very brave little girl. I wish we all could feel so brave."

Turning to her mother-in-law, Jochebed says, "I am so happy the midwives are not going to kill any children, but Horus' eye sees everything. How long will it be before the Pharaoh knows Puah and Shiphrah are not doing as he ordered them? I am worried. Tirzah's baby is due very soon. Can we trust so many women to keep quiet? Someone always lets a secret slip out."

"Have faith, child. Pray that the babies will be safe. All we can do now is have faith in the Almighty," Mahala says quietly.

Jochebed sits on the wool blanket. She pulls Aaron onto her crossed legs and offers the eagerly—waiting child her breast. "I thought it was hard when the Egyptians wanted to take our crops and supplies, Now I know what real worry is. Surely the children will be safe. There must be a way to keep them safe."

TAWERET GODDESS OF CHILDBIRTH

In Egyptian culture, prayers to Taweret were considered essential in giving birth. The goddess was shown as a pregnant hippopotamus with characteristics of a crocodile. Her ferocious appearance helped her to keep evil from attacking the birthing mother.

Chapter 6:
The Late-Night Tragedy

"Come down, placenta, come down! Look, Hathor will lay her hand on her with an amulet of health!" An Egyptian chant for Hathor, the goddess of childbirth.

Flickering shadows dance across the bovine face of the great stone statue of Hathor, the cow Goddess. A kindly deity believed to protect women in childbirth, she stares placidly at the busy scene in the temple birth house. Excitement builds as an Egyptian prince is soon to be born.

Evil spirits, demons, and bad luck are kept at bay by the fierce hippopotamus Goddess, Taweret. Taweret's image is a carved wooden image standing near the birthing chair. Her presence is considered essential to a successful birth.

The thick smell of spicy incense emanating from burning oil in lamps attached to the wall fills the room with hazy smoke. Musicians, dancers, and singers perform the chants and incantations to the goddesses pleading with them to drive away all negative forces so that a healthy child may be welcomed into the world. The music becomes louder as the performers anticipate the prospective mother's anguished cries.

Midwives, dressed in loin cloths, and their helpers are scurrying about readying for the arrival of the royal prince. Meryt, the favorite daughter of Pharaoh and Queen Nephre, is in labor. Her child should make its appearance before the sun rises.

Nailah, the first assistant to the head midwife, has been keeping a careful watch on the progress of the impending birth. She frequently examines the progress, as she assures the princess all is going well.

Nailah looks across the room and sees Sheba, the head midwife, motioning for a conference with her.

"Have her get on the birthing bricks and start pushing," Sheba says as Nailah comes near.

"My lady," Naila answers, "She is not ready for pushing. She has more time to go before the pushing should start. Pushing too early could be bad for the baby."

"She is ready. The Queen will be here soon. She will be very happy to see the baby when she arrives. This birth has been long anticipated. She is not a patient person. Start the pushing process."

"The baby is not ready to move down. We must wait a little longer."

"Do not question me! Move her to the birthing bricks!"

Nailah helps Meryt move to the elaborately decorated bricks and assume a deep squat with her feet on unfired clay birthing bricks. The princess, a slender and somewhat fragile girl, grasps two cloth ropes that hang from the ceiling. She pulls against the ropes as she squats and pushes down with her stomach muscles to move her preborn child into the birth canal.

Her thin linen dress is soon soaked in sweat. Her black hair hangs in strings down her back. Perspiration drips from the ends of the hair strands. Her face is pale and her knuckles are white from grasping the ropes. Each push brings an intense, pain-filled scream from the princess.

Nailah motions for the princess to stop pushing so she can examine the progress of the birth. She immediately steps away to consult with Sheba.

"My lady, something is going wrong. She must stop pushing now. The baby is not moving down anymore. What shall we do?"

Sheba, a thin, middle-aged woman with a nervous habit of twitching her nose, says, wringing her hands, "What has happened?" she asks.

"I'm not sure, but it looks like the baby has not moved, even though she is pushing very hard."

"Why did you have her on the birthing brick? It is too early for her to push."

Nailah retorts, "She is on the bricks because you told me it was time for her to push."

Sheba points her finger and shakes it toward Nailah's face. "Stop questioning me! No! I did not say it was time for her to push. You moved her to the bricks without my permission. It was too early for her to push. You moved her without permission. Do you understand?"

Nailah's face flushes as anger flames into her eyes. She clamps her mouth shut and mutters through clenched teeth. "I understand."

Sheba turns on her heel and walks away.

Naila returns to the princess.

"Lady Meryt, we will move you to the birthing chair. We see you are getting very tired. The chair will hold you up more comfortably." Motioning for her teenage apprentice, they move the princess to the birthing chair.

Moving out of earshot of the princess, Nailah whispers to the girl, "Go as fast as you can run. Call the African to come immediately."

Sheba whispers to the queen's serving maid, Nuti, "What must we do? What can we do? This is very bad!"

Sheba twists a scarf in her hands. Her eyes dart around the room.

"Stop fretting. We haven't lost her yet. You always give up so easily. You cannot afford to lose this one by being too nervous." Nuti says trying to remain calm.

Nailah approaches Sheba. "Madam Sheba, I must speak to you."

Nailah waves toward the door motioning toward a small, dark female slave who stands at the door accompanied by the apprentice. The slave comes to Nailah. Her full lips open in a smile that reveal shining white teeth that glow against her dark face.

"What do you want?" Sheba snaps.

"This lady has helped me save four mothers and their babies when the birth became difficult. Before she was taken from her tribe by Pharaoh's soldiers, she was a skilled midwife. The women of her tribe are slender like many of our women. Her grandmother taught her how to position the baby, so birth comes smoothly. Even slender women in her tribe give birth to large babies. These children often become mighty warriors. She herself has given birth to three strong men. Will you listen to what she has to say?"

The lamp light casts highlights of deep blue tones on the woman's shining ebony skin. Short curls of kinky hair cling close to her scalp. Sheba stares at the woman with a disdainful, downturned mouth.

"Mighty warriors you say. Don't you know Pharaoh's armies overran the villages of Eastern Africa? If they were such mighty warriors, why were they slaves in Egypt? I will not allow a captured slave to touch Pharaoh's daughter. Send her out of this room!" Sheba turns her back and walks away.

Tears come to Naliah's eyes and stream down her cheeks. She wipes them away with a cloth before going to Meryt's side. Occasionally she steps away when the tears start again as the princess continues to tire.

As midnight nears Meryt has been in labor for almost six hours. The young woman slumps on the birthing chair succumbing to the intense pain and fatigue. Two midwife helpers kneel behind the princess supporting her limp body. Two others, one on each side, support her arms. Her head falls on her chest. A long moan escapes her lips. Nuti scurries to the helpless woman with a plaster of sea salt and emmer wheat. She places it on the princess's swollen belly to ease the pain.

Other midwife attendants gather around. They sponge her forehead and rub her back trying to ease the excruciating pain. The baby has moved down into the birth canal but can go no further.

Four women, dressed in transparent, fine linen costumes sporting elaborate collars depicting symbols of their gods, chant as they dance and clap to the music of drums and a sacred rattle called a systrum. "Come down, placenta, come down! Look, Hathor will lay her hand on her with an amulet of health!"

They repeat this four times as they place the image of Bes on the laboring woman's brow while more and more intense incantations and prayers are chanted.

Suddenly, Queen Nephre bursts into the room followed by Titi. "How are things going? Has the baby come yet? Why is it taking so long?

The midwives look up and freeze in awkward poses.

When Nephre sees her daughter barely conscious, she screams at the midwives, "What happened?! What have you done to her? She is unconscious! Do something now! I command you!"

The queen slings her hands and paces the floor. "You absolutely must not let my daughter die! Does anyone here know what to do?".

Sheba approaches the queen cautiously. "Your majesty, we are doing all we can do. We have the images of the sacred gods here with us. We have said the sacred chants and evoked the gracious, powerful Hathor to give her strength. We called for Bes to drive off the demons. The baby is not moving. She is so weak she cannot push anymore. We are doing all that is possible to save her."

"Nonsense! Look! My daughter is dying right before my eyes, and you are doing nothing! I will have your head if she dies. I will die too. Why would I want to live without my daughter?! She is my life! Now do something! I am commanding you!" the Queen yells hysterically.

"Your Highness, Hathor does not favor us!" Sheba pleads. "If the great goddess does not favor us, what can we do to change her mind? Young women often die in childbirth. You cannot blame us. We are doing all we know to do."

"Then you are idiots! What you know is not enough! If all you can do is stand there and make excuses, it is not enough! I am losing her, and all you do is stand there!" shouts Nephre as she frantically waves her hands.

Titi whispers to Nuti, "If only the Hebrew midwives were here. They are the most successful midwives in Egypt. Very few Hebrew children are lost." Titi immediately clasps her hand over her mouth.

Nuti's face twists out of shape. Her eyebrows go up sharply. She pulls her lips tight, so no words come out.

"What did you say?" demands the Queen. "I heard you say something. What did you say?"

"It was nothing important," Titi says twisting her hands and pulling on her thumb.

"You did say something important! I heard only part of it. What was it? Answer me now!"

"I only said that the Hebrew midwives seem to deliver children without trouble. It was a foolish thing to say. Forgive me, your Highness."

"Go at once and call the Hebrew midwives to come immediately!"

"Your Majesty, the king will be angry!" Titi responds with horror. "We are forbidden to call Hebrews to the temple birth house. Besides, it is very dark tonight. Demons are roaming in the streets."

"Demons be damned forever in the dark hell! Let the King battle them. That is his job! I don't care about demons. The Pharaoh will not have to know. If our daughter and her baby die, he surely will be in a rage. Hebrews, Egyptians, Nubians! Can any of them save my daughter? Do I care if they are slaves, kings, or shepherds? If any one of them can save my daughter, I will be ecstatically happy. Go now and get the Hebrew midwives!"

Waving her hand above her head, pointing toward the door, Nephre screams, stamping her foot. "Go now before I throw you and everyone else into the prison house."

Titi falls to the floor begging, "Please, please, do not make me go out in the dark! The demons will tear out my eyes and eat me alive! I will be cursed forever!"

"Stop it. Stop that blubbering! If you do not do as I say, you will be begging the demons to eat you. You will think the demons are merciful if my daughter dies! Go now. Take Nuti with you. Get horses from the stables. Here is the silver." The Queen pulls out a small bag of silver coins which she always carries under her dress.

Handing some of them to Titi, she orders, "Now go! Hurry!" Titi takes the coins which she will use to bribe the stable master. She rises and leaves on her mission.

Nephre paces around the room becoming more agitated. "All of you musicians, chanters, and singers leave! Now! I am tired of all this wracking noise! Get out of here! Everyone except the midwives must go now! If I hear a peep from any of you, you will spend the rest of your life in a dark prison. If you say a word about any of this to anyone, you will surely regret it for the rest of your short life! Understand? I mean everything I say! You had better listen to everything I say!"

After what seems like an eternity there is a timid knock on the outer door. When the door opens a crack, Titi and Nuti followed by Shiphrah and Puah are bidden to enter. The Egyptian midwives step back to allow the Hebrew women near the suffering princess.

The Queen points toward her daughter, "Save her! Please save her. I beg you I will do what you want me to do. Just save my daughter." She stands aside grasping her hands in anguish.

Surveying the situation, the midwives go to work with the unconscious young women. They quickly determine the problem.

Puah nods toward Shiphrah, speaking in Hebrew. "She is like many Egyptian women who have narrow hips. It is difficult to push a baby out with so narrow hips. She pushed before the baby was ready to move. Now she is exhausted and unconscious from so much pushing. It is necessary to get the baby out, or she will die. We must be very gentle. I will push for her. You will have to pull the baby out."

Pushing and pulling gently at the right places, little by little, the two experienced women guide the infant out of the birth canal with great difficulty. Finally, the small limp body slides into Shiphrah's hands. Shiphrah holds up the lifeless body of the child in the glow of the lamplight.

Nephre's shoulders slump. Her neck seems to give way as her head lowers toward her chest. Tears stream down her face. She motions for Sheba to bring the baby to her. Sheba takes the body and wraps it in the elaborately-decorated linen and silk wraps prepared by his mother for him to wear on his first day of life. The cheerful wraps have become his shroud.

Nephre stretches out trembling hands to receive the little bundle. Her lower lip trembles as she looks at the tiny doll's face. Speaking to him between choking sobs, she says "Mose, precious son. Mose, you have left us! Why have you left us? You are so handsome! You were supposed to grow into a powerful king! But you have left us."

She stokes the tiny face, blue from lack of oxygen, and traces his perfect little nose. "Since the day your coming was announced, your mother has talked about nothing but you. She was so joyful when she knew about your coming. What is left for her now? Must she watch someone else produce a son to sit on Pharaoh's throne? Or will she go with you to the land of no return?"

She clasps the baby to her breast and weeps rocking back and forth, I still pouring out her grief.

"And what will I do? Will I lose everything? Mose, ahh, dear Mose, you have left us desolate. My heart is broken! My heart is broken…."

The women in the room remain silent with eyes on the floor. No one moves.

Meryt raises her hand slightly as she moans softly. The Hebrew midwives move to her side. They examine her. They rub pain-relieving herbs onto her skin as they massage her arms and legs.

Quietly Sheba slinks out to the corridor followed by Nuti who softly shuts the door behind her. Sheba wrings her hands and grasps her hair.

"The Queen will be displeased with me! I could not save her grandson, and her daughter may die too. I did not know how to get the baby out. If the princess dies, I will lose my position! How horrible! Oh! How horrible. If she lives, everyone will know those stinking Hebrew women did what I could not do. I am disgraced! I will be a destitute woman. The queen will drive me from the palace, and I will live in poverty for the rest of my life. I will have to carry firewood or even worse!"

Her face twists into a wicked mask.

"Why did that stupid girl mention the Hebrew midwives? If I am turned out of the palace, I will put an adder in her bed! I know where to get all kinds of poisonous snakes! She should have kept her stupid mouth shut. She will not get away with this!" Clenching her teeth, she pounds her fist against the wall.

"No, this is not true!" Nuti attempts to calm her.

Nuti has survived the palace intrigue that continuously lies in wait to trap the unwary at an unguarded moment. Her uncanny ability to navigate the turbulent political waters, stirred by the erratic fickle whims of a paranoid Pharaoh has allowed her to survive where many others have failed.

Nuti wraps her arm around Sheba's shoulders. "Calm down. You will not lose your place in the palace. The queen will not tell Pharaoh anything about the Hebs. She will not want him to know she called these low-class women near the temple birth house. She could be in huge trouble for disobeying the king. She will tell him nothing. She will not do anything to you because it would bring disaster on herself."

"How can you be so sure?" Sheba asks doubtfully.

"She could lose her position as the Queen. We will never tell the king or any of his men what really happened. We will tell all the women who were present in the birthing room to keep this quiet, or we will report them to the Queen. The Queen has said what she will do if they do not obey her. They know she can be terrible when she is angry. These awful events of this night are secrets only women need to know."

"What if someone tells the Queen I did not listen to Nailah when she said the African slave woman could save the baby?

Nuti puts her hands firmly on Sheba's shoulders, her face close to Sheba's. Her dark eyes seem to grow darker, and her sharp nose seems to grow longer. The birthmark on her forehead gets darker as she speaks,

"You do not know whether that woman could have saved the baby. Neither does anyone else. Hear me! If anyone asks about the death of the child, just say it could not be helped because the gods did not favor the birth. This is all you must do. But you will never have to answer that question. Babies die during the birthing process every day. Why would the king ask any more questions? He does not know anything about how women give birth. Who will tell him? You are his expert. Do you understand?"

Sheba is skeptical. "How do you know all this? This can get us sold into slavery. How can you be so sure it will not come back to trap us?"

Nuti is more forceful. "Trust me. Be calm and keep your thoughts in check. You will never have to worry if you do not make foolish assumptions that will cause you to act with fear. Fear is your worst enemy. People read fear. Then they start to ask questions. We must stick together on our story. This is the way we survive in this palace. Remember what I say."

Shiphrah and Puah leave before dawn approaches. They must avoid being seen by Pharaoh's priests who will soon be on the streets to begin their morning duties. The women exit the birth house by a back door and slip away quietly into the dark. The thin sliver of a waning moon gives enough light to find the path toward the village.

"Do you think the princess will live?" asks Puah when they had traveled a few miles away from the city.

Shiphrah responds slowly, "I am not sure. Egyptian women are delicate. Childbirth is often hard for them. Pray to God she does live. If she lives it may help us save our own children. It is too bad we could not save the baby. If we could have come earlier, we may have been able to save him. If both had lived, the queen and princess might have favored us and asked the king to pardon us for disobeying him."

Struggling to figure out the situation, Shiphrah muses, "If she dies, we may have to face the terrible punishment sooner than we thought. These

Egyptian women may even blame us for the death of the princess and her baby. Prayer is our only hope to get through this."

Chapter 7:
Unwitting Collaboration

He will make your righteous reward shine like the dawn,
your vindication like the noonday sun.
Psalms 37:6

Shiphrah and Puah lean against the wall in a small room in Pharaoh's Great House. A guard is posted outside the door. Faces white with fear, they communicate only in low whispers.

"Puah's face is ashen; her voice trembles as she speaks, "Grandma was terrified when they came for me. They left two guards at my house to watch her and the children. They wanted to make sure no one could leave or come in. Two men walked with me all the way. What will happen to my children? Will I ever see them again? Do you think they will believe our story?"

Shiphrah's voice shakes with dread. "Our only hope is that they do believe us. I do not think they will want to accept anything we tell them. They really do not want to believe us. They think our people are strong, and they need to control us, so they may look for reasons to punish us. It seems they kept close count of the number of children born since we were here almost two years ago."

After hours pass, Fazel appears suddenly. Gone is the broad smile and friendly manner. With a very serious face, he stands, arms crossed, looking down at them.

"Ladies, didn't the Pharaoh give you a great party? He was willing to make your dreams come true, yet you have failed him. I am in trouble because I told our Great King you are his friends, and you were willing to do anything he wanted. Now look what trouble you have caused me. I must tell him you failed. And I thought you were my friends, I do not want to see you or your families hurt, so what must I tell the Pharaoh?" He asks sternly.

Puah lowers her head and keeps her eyes on the floor as if she were trying to disappear into the wall. She stifles a sob. But Shiphrah draws a breath and pulls her shoulders up, looking into the man's eyes as if she is his equal. She holds him with her unwavering gaze as her eyes continue to focus on him, and she speaks resolutely without a tremble in her voice.

"Please forgive our miserable failures. We beg mercy from our Great Pharaoh. Please tell him we could not do what he wanted."

As she takes a deep breath, her eyes focus more intently on him; her words become more pressing.

"We are returning His Lordship's gold because we could not do as he asked." She holds up a pouch containing the gold jewelry received at their last visit to the Great House.

"You see, it is not easy to help Hebrew women with childbirth. Our women work hard in the fields during planting and harvesting seasons. In building season, they carry bricks to help build Pharaoh's projects. They are very strong and especially fit. As you know, they have but a few days to give birth to their baby and be back at work. They need little help with childbirth. By the time we or our helpers arrive at the house, the baby has already arrived and is in the arms of its father."

The eunuch draws back a bit and crosses his arms. His eyebrows knit at the center.

Shiphrah continues. "You see it is not our fault. We just could not do what the great Pharaoh asked us to do. Here is his gold; we must return it because we were not able to earn it. Please ask for his Lordship's mercy on us. We will be forever grateful to you." She pushes the pouch of gold toward him.

Fazel's eyebrows go up sharply. Shocked by her boldness, he stares at the little woman for a moment as if to take in all she said. He grabs the pouch from her hand as he turns to leave.

"I will inform His Lordship. Perhaps, he will accept your story. Perhaps not!"

Fazel reports to Pharaoh all Shiphrah said to him. He waits for the king's response.

The king listens to the story as he is enjoying his afternoon snack. On hearing the report, he yells and stabs his knife into the wooden table. "What kind of stupid nonsense is this?"

The king's face turns a bright red as a vein in his forehead visibly stands out. His lips puff as if he is attempting to blow up a balloon. He shouts, "Do those ugly stinking cows take me for a fool? How dare they bring me this foolishness! Are they really this stupid? Only an idiot would return gold!" As he pounds the arm of his chair with his fist, he bellows, "Do you think there is any truth to this tale?"

"I'm not sure, Your Lordship. She did return the gold, and she seemed very sincere." Fazel puts the pouch full of gold on the table in front of Pharaoh.

The king opens the ties and turns the bag upside down. The jewelry falls clattering on the table. With a forceful swipe of his hand, he sends it flying onto the floor.

Fazel says with measured calmness, "Would His Majesty like me to call Sheba? She knows all about childbirth since she has helped with many births at this court. She will tell us if this is a lie or if is there any truth to this story."

"Yes! Just get her here as soon as possible! If this is a pack of lies, those filthy sows will wish they had never seen a baby." The king pops a raisin cake in his mouth and washes it down with wine. He hacks the last two pieces of cake into small bits and smashes them on the table.

"Idiots! Idiots! All I ever deal with is idiots! Just spare me from idiots!" he shouts as he pounds his fist on the table.

The king's messenger arrives at Sheba's door and knocks, "Who is it?"

Sheba asks as she peeks through the small opening.

"His Royal Highness commands you to appear before him at once." the messenger orders.

"Why does the Pharaoh want me to come?" She opens the door a slight bit more.

"He needs your knowledge about childbirth. Be quick! Don't keep him waiting! He is not in a good mood," the messenger says.

A shock travels the length of Sheba's body. "Please allow me a few minutes to dress properly before presenting myself before His Lordship. I will be there very shortly."

Closing the door, she listens until she can no longer hear his footsteps. She opens the door and looks down the corridor. Satisfied he has gone, she dashes down the hall to find Nuti in the queen's dressing room folding the queen's clothing. Glancing right and left she makes sure no one is in the room or the adjoining rooms.

Satisfied they are alone, she wails, "Oh, Nuti, what will I do? What can I say? Pharaoh is going to ask me about what happened to his grandson! Someone must have told him about the Heb midwives and the slave woman. What will I say? Help me! What if he blames me for his grandson's death? Please, please, help me!" she begs, sinking to her knees with her hands clasped in front of her face.

"Stop it! Calm down! You must be calm. How do you know that is the reason he is calling you? Stand up!" Nuti takes her hand and raises her off the floor.

Sheba wrings her hands when she is standing. "There is no other reason why the Pharaoh would call me. The messenger said Pharaoh needs my knowledge about childbirth. He doesn't call on women unless it is very, very important. It must be about what happened that terrible night."

Nuti places her hands firmly on Sheba's shoulders shaking them slightly as she looks into her eyes with calculating intensity. The brown blotch of a birthmark above her left eyebrow turns red.

"Listen to me! I told you this before. Now listen to me! Who would have told him anything about that night? You and I did not tell him. The Queen certainly did not tell him. I don't think any of the women would leak the story. They know they would be endangering their own lives."

Nuti's voice takes a more urgent tone. "The king does not know anything about what happened. Stay with your story! Remember I told you to make no foolish assumptions! Be calm and answer only the questions he asks you. Do not act guilty or admit any fault. Just say the gods did not favor the birth. Do this and you will be alright. If you do everything I say, you will be ok. Do you understand?"

Nuti gives the shoulders a final firm shake. "Now go!"

Sheba stands very still for a moment staring at the red blotch on Nuti's forehead. She slowly nods affirmatively then hurries to find Fazel waiting near the dining room. She kneels before him keeping her eyes on the floor.

"His Gracious Lordship has called me? What is his pleasure? What can your humble servant do for his Lordship? I am always ready to serve Egypt's king."

Fazel ushers her into the king's presence. Sheba kneels on the floor and bows to touch her forehead to the tile.

"Your Lordship," Fazel addresses the King, "Sheba is here to answer your questions."

The king does not acknowledge Sheba. He motions for his wine taster to pour another cup of wine and taste it. After a proper time, he is satisfied the wine is safe to drink. He grabs the cup and washes down the last of his snacks. With a loud grunt, he signals Fazel to begin his questions.

"Sheba, you have helped many women in the Great House give birth to babies. Do you consider yourself to have much knowledge about childbirth?" Fazel queries.

Sheba raises her head, keeping her eyes on the floor while remaining on her knees.

"Yes. I have served His Lordship's court for many years. I have seen many children born. His Lordship's daughter and many other children safely entered this great kingdom with my help."

Sheba feels her heart pounding as her chest muscles tighten around her ribs. She clasps her hands together so hard the knuckles are white.

"Now explain to His Lordship, does the safe birth of a child depend on the skill of the midwife, or is a successful birth dependent on the health and strength of mother and child?"

Sheba draws a very deep breath. Choosing her words carefully she says, "Some of our women have trouble bringing their children into the world. If a woman is strong, she can usually give birth without a lot of trouble, but if she has a weakness, or the gods do not favor her, she may lose her baby because the process of birthing is very difficult. The baby may die before it can be born. There is nothing anyone can do about it." She pauses, waiting for his response.

Fazel is silent for a moment stroking his chin. "What about Hebrew women? Are their midwives more skilled than our own midwives or are the Hebrew women healthier?"

Sheba feels the blood drain from her face. Forgetting Nuti's admonitions to keep calm, she blurts out. "Those Hebrew cows have butts as big as horses! They can squirt a baby out like a nanny goat! They squat at the edge of a grain field and with a push or two out comes the little bastard! Those hags don't know how to do anything. They would not know what to do in a difficult birth situation. I am glad they do not try to bring Egyptian children into this world. That would be a disaster!"

Fazel's chin drops as his eyebrows go up. He shakes his head from side to side then dismisses her with a wave of his hand. "You have said enough. Go!"

Sheba rises from her knees and leaves as quickly as she dares.

Throwing his knife at the wall, the king roars with frustration. The knife smacks the stone wall bouncing back toward the king. It narrowly misses hitting Fazel, who jumps aside before it falls clattering on the floor.

"What stupid idiots these Hebrew cows are! That fool of a priest did not do his homework! These incompetent whores are too stupid to know a command even from a king. It is like trying to issue a command to the frogs in the river! Get an order to General Anherkhau! I need a military man to handle this situation!"

"Will you punish the midwives, My Lord?"

"What would be the use? Will it make them any smarter? Send them away so I won't have to see or smell them. They have already cost too much time and resources. Forget them! Let's get on with this project!"

Chapter 8:
Red Paint on the Gate and the Soothsayer's Warning

"Her majesty Isis shines into the temple on New Year's Day, and she mingles her light with that of her father Ra on the horizon." From the ancient temple of Isis-Hathor at Denderah, Egypt

When Shiphrah and Puah returned from the Great House unharmed but shaken, there was great rejoicing that lasted a short time and then turned to dread and apprehension as more and more questions arose about what could be in store for the children. No one believes the king will abandon his plan to control the number of male children. Everyone is on edge waiting for the dreaded news of a new plan.

Weeks pass. Suddenly one morning chariots appear in the village. They go from house to house stopping at each home to survey it. Soldiers carrying containers of red ochre paint jump out of the chariots and splatter the paint on gateposts of selected houses.

When the last chariot disappears, Sarah and Jochebed survey the eerie splash of red on their gatepost. The ominous sign sends a haunting chill up the spine. What could it mean?

"This looks like dried blood! I know it is only paint, but it almost looks like someone died here. Why did they put this paint on our gate? See, they did not put any on that gate or on that house across the path. What are they doing?" Sarah asks puzzled.

"I know what it is about," Jochebed says with a shudder, as the truth starts to dawn on her. "They wanted Shiphrah and Puah to kill the male children. Since they did not do it, they are planning another way to kill the children. There is not a male baby living in the house across the path so there is no paint on it. They know Aaron lives here. They are not only going after the newborns but the nursing babies as well." She draws her breath in. "What will I do? They will be coming for Aaron!" she whispers in a voice of panic.

"The taskmasters are not interested in children. They are interested in men who can work. Those two houses have elderly people living there. I think they are interested in the men. The paint must have to do with counting strong workers. Amram is very strong. They are selecting him for a work project," Sarah says, as she wraps her arms across her bosom, "There could be a lot of reasons they would mark the houses."

Jochebed is cold with fear. Her voice trembles as she speaks, "The Egyptians always keep records of everything. We had to report Aaron's birth. They know about all the babies in this village, except the ones the mothers are hiding since Shiphrah and Puah told us not to report the new births. Somehow, they found out all the births were not being reported. Now they are going to do something to our children. "Pharaoh sent his soldiers to splash this paint on the gates. Do you think we can hide from them? If they know everything, where is there to hide? How can I hide Aaron from soldiers?"

"Sarah attempts to soothe her fears. "There is surely another reason why they put this paint on our gate. Soldiers fight battles. They do not count babies. It looks spooky, but there must be another reason for the paint."

The following day, Jochebed, Sarah, and Ana are walking toward the city pulling a cart loaded with baskets to be sold in the Egyptian marketplace.

Ana steadies the baskets on the cart. "We need to keep our ears open. Maybe we can hear something about what is going to happen. There is always someone connected with the palace willing to talk. Egyptians do not keep secrets very well. Every time I come to the market a woman is there who tells all she knows to anyone who will listen. Sometimes I do not know if everything she says is true. I think she has relatives who work in the palace. She may know someone who knows about the paint."

"Any information is valuable. We must get an idea of what they're planning." Sarah, trying to sound hopeful, looks toward Jochebed. Jochebed says nothing. Nervously, she plays with the bracelet on her wrist. Her breaths are shallow. She is paying little attention to the conversation. It appears every step she takes is an effort. Since the paint appeared on the gatepost, she has spoken only a few words.

Sarah tries again to reassure Jochebed to no avail. "You look as if all is lost. Aaron is safe at home with his grandmother as always. Cheer up. You will not be able to think clearly if you do not eat or sleep. Aaron is in no danger now,"

Jochebed simply looks at her sister-in-law blankly and says nothing.

The marketplace is a seething, moving mass of bodies packed closely around every vendor's booth. Egyptians from all over the kingdom are searching for many kinds of items in preparation for the approaching festival. After searching out a spot, the women set up the basket display amid the surging throng of shoppers. Buying is brisk and the supply of baskets dwindles rapidly.

When there is a lull in the activity, Jochebed says suddenly, "I need to get some olive oil for Mahala. I saw a booth with oils as we came in. I will be right back in a minute." She turns toward the street.

"Wait a little while until these last baskets are sold and we will go with you. You do not need to be alone in this market. You know how dangerous it is for a woman to be alone," Sarah warns.

Jochebed turns to go. "I will be alright. I just need to walk. I am feeling so nervous I want to go now. Do not worry. I will be just fine."

Sarah pleads with her. "I do not want you to go. We can't leave Ana here alone; thieves will bully her and steal our money and our baskets. Please wait for us, Honey. Don't make me worry about you even more than I am already."

"That's right," Ana says supporting Sarah. "You shouldn't be going anywhere in this market alone. We can't take the chance that our baskets, our carts, or our money will be stolen. We will go with you as soon as we sell these last baskets."

"I do not want you to worry; it will be easier for me to get the olive oil alone. We won't have to pull this cart through the crowd. I will be just fine." With that, she quickly goes down the street and is lost in the sea of moving humanity.

Jochebed struggles through the crowd. First, she looks at one booth, then another. Her eyes rest on an elaborate booth where various images of Egyptian gods, amulets, scented oil, and many other items for fortune-telling are on display. She is drawn to the booth. She stands contemplating the merchandise when a hard bump on her shoulder startles her.

"Oh, excuse me, dear. I did not mean to bump into you so hard. It must be fate that brings you here so close to my booth."

When Jochebed turns to see who is speaking, she is staring into the elaborately painted eyes of an Egyptian soothsayer. The woman is wearing a large black wig and very big earrings. Colorful robes drape her body. Her fingers are covered with many kinds of jeweled rings.

Did I hear you say you are worried about your son?" the soothsayer asks knowingly.

"How did you know? How can you know that? You do not know me. I have never seen you before," Jochebed stammers.

The soothsayer holds up an image of a scarab beetle carved from green jade.

"I know everything. Khepri, the beetle, tells me everything. Is there anything you want to know?" The many bracelets on her arms jingle with her every move. The soothsayer turns her head to the side and gives Jochebed a side-long look as if she is hiding a secret.

The young mother frantically begs. "Do you know what I can do to save my son? I must know. I just must know! It is making me sick with worry."

"So, you believe your son is in danger?" the black-wigged woman asks. " You are right to fear for your son's life. He is in very great danger. What will you give me to tell you what the wise beetle says? What would you give in exchange for your son's life?"

Jochebed's heart leaps. The color bleaches from her face. She feels the choking fear bind tighter around her rib cage and the hair prickle on her neck. She gasps.

"I have nothing to give. We brought baskets and sold them. We got some money, but most of it is not mine. I have some copper pieces I was going to spend on olive oil. We have a few baskets left. Do you want the baskets and this copper?" Jochebed desperately says.

"No. Your son is surely worth more than a few baskets and this small amount of copper. Will you trade anything you own for your son's life?" Again, the soothsayer appears to be wise and knowledgeable.

"If I could, I would give all I have to save my son, but I have nothing. Believe me, I have nothing. I would give it to you if I had money."

"You do have something. You have a bracelet on your arm. I will take that." The soothsayer gives her another sidelong glance.

"This is my wedding bracelet. It has been passed down for many generations of my family. I can't give this. My daughter will wear it when she is married. You can't have it," Jochebed says flatly.

"So, you value a bracelet more than your son's life, do you? Well then. Keep it. I won't tell you anything." The soothsayer turns to leave.

"Wait! I must know. I will give you my bracelet. Here it is. Now tell me." Jochebed takes the bracelet from her arm and hands it to the woman.

Taking the bracelet and examining it with pleasure, the soothsayer puts it on her arm with the many other bracelets.

She goes to a colorful woven mat where she assumes a sitting position with her legs crossed in front of her. Her eyes roll upward. She puts her hands together over her nose, still holding the jade beetle, closing her eyes; mumbling sounds and semi-words come from her lips as if she is receiving a revelation.

In slow, drawn-out sentences, she chants.

"Beware the Star of Isis. When its light strikes the Queen, I see grave danger to Abraham's children. Hear the horses! See the blood! On that terrible day run! Run! Run fast as you dare. Away, away from the blood!"

She waits for a long pause. "This is your warning. I can see no more."

"This is all you can tell me?" Jochebed's voice is a shrill shriek.

"This is what you need to know," the soothsayer declares.

Frantic, Jochebed screams. "I gave my bracelet to you! You have not told me anything. Give my bracelet back to me now! I want it back right now! You do not know anything. You are a thief! You just stole my bracelet!"

Rising off the mat, the soothsayer says, "A deal is a deal. You traded your bracelet for a revelation. You have the revelation, dear. Use it wisely. Goodbye."

She steps into the crowded street and disappears into the sea of bodies.

Stunned, feeling violated, and faint Jochebed begins to weep.

"How could I be so stupid? I knew that woman was a thief! Why did I give her my beautiful bracelet? What will I tell Amram? What about Father? He will be so disappointed with me! What will I tell Mahala? I am so stupid!" She falls to her knees in the street, crying loudly as if her heart will break.

In a short while, gentle hands are lifting her up out of the dirty street, brushing off the dirt from her clothes, soothing her hair, and asking questions of genuine concern. Ana and Sarah have found her.

"Are you hurt? What has happened? We have been looking for you. I knew something bad would happen if you went alone. Tell us, are you hurt.?" Sarah is hugging her tightly.

The young woman's sobs come more vigorously. Ashamed and distraught, she gasps, "No, ah…my arm hurts. My bracelet is gone. It's gone! My beautiful bracelet is gone!" she sobs.

"There, there, tell us what has happened," Sarah says, stroking Jochebed's hair.

"Some... I think it was some Egyptian teenage boys who came and demanded my bracelet. They pulled it off my arm," Jochebed lies. "I was so afraid of them. Please don't tell Amram, Mahala, or anyone else. I was so foolish to go alone. I should have listened to you. Please promise me you won't tell," she pleads.

"We promise we won't tell. There. There. You are lucky you are not hurt. I'm so sorry about your bracelet. That is a great loss, but it could have been so much worse. We will not tell anyone you lost the bracelet. You can tell them when you feel better," Ana croons.

"You are so good. Thank you. Thank you. Sarah and Ana, what would I ever do without you two?"

The lie makes her feel very guilty. Their complete faith in her truthfulness makes her feel even worse.

"Are you able to walk home?" Sarah asks. Jochebed nods affirmative.

"Then let's go. It is getting late. All the baskets are sold. We did very well with our sales today. The buyers seem to like the most colorful ones best."

When they are some distance from the city, Jochebed recovers her composure.

"Sarah, what is the Star of Isis? Why do the Egyptians celebrate so wildly at the river?"

Sarah looks at her sister-in-law confused. "The Star of Isis? Why do you ask about that? You know about the Star of Isis."

"I know they have a festival that they celebrate wildly. We always look forward to getting time away from work because they are celebrating, I have not heard very much about why they are celebrating except there are a lot of drunken parties. Please tell me why they are so happy at this festival. Go over it slowly," Jochebed says.

Sarah looks at Ana who looks back at her with a questioning look.

Sarah begins, "They are preparing to celebrate very soon. It is a signal the New Year has arrived. Sometimes the star is called the Dog Star. But when the light from the star falls on a jewel that is placed on the forehead of the statue of their goddess queen, the priest says the New Year has arrived, and Pharaoh declares the celebration."

When she pauses, Ana takes up the narrative.

"We know the festival is near when we see the river rising. They start cooking and making a lot of beer. Sometimes we can smell it if the wind is in the right direction. There will be so many people along the river you cannot get past them. Pharaoh's golden barge carries their shrine down the river while Pharaoh sacrifices to their gods and the people cheer him. They play music, drink, and dance for many hours. They return home and have more parties. For days they do not work; they only have fun. You know all this. You have seen it many times. We always bring our baskets to sell before the festival. Why are you asking if you know these things?

"Yes. I know all this, but I am trying to think what this could mean for us. The red paint on our gate must have something to do with this festival. Why would they mark certain houses? What does this festival mean to the Egyptians?" Jochebed persists.

Ana continues her narrative. "When the river is rising, it brings hope for a season of good grain crops. They celebrate the coming of the water because the water means good crops and abundant food for the coming year. They offer many sacrifices with the hope their gods will bring a bountiful year. They say this new year is a rebirth and a renewal of life. This is their festival where the most sacrifices are offered This is their worship and praise to their many gods. They say their gods demand their worship and sacrifices."

"What sacrifices do they offer?" Jochebed asks.

"I'm not sure. Maybe wine, fruit, or grain. They offer meat from different animals, which they give to the crocodiles who represent their gods that live in the sacred river."

A horrible thought strikes Jochebed. The idea is so inconceivable she dares not express it. As she pushes the idea out of her mind, a shiver runs up her spine. She feels faint. Her knees start to bend as she stumbles before catching herself.

"Are you alright?" Sarah and Ana say at the same time as they grab her arms to prevent her fall.

"When did you say the celebrating starts?" Jochebed asks with a shaky voice when she regains her feet.

"It starts tomorrow. Why do you ask?"

"The festival is a very big event for the Egyptians. They are marking our house with red paint. It is very disturbing. I want to wash the paint off, but I have been afraid to do it. I am going to wash it off when we get home."

"No!" Sarah says emphatically. "Don't do that! They would punish Amram. He would take a severe beating. Do you want him to be beaten? I do not want you to wash the paint off. It could be dangerous for all of us. Leave it alone! Don't cause more trouble to come on us."

Later that night when the family has settled in, Jochebed alone is awake. Amram is snoring peacefully as if he is catching up on some much-needed rest. Mahala sleeps near Miriam and Aaron. Sarah is curled on a sheep's skin and covered with a blanket in the far corner of the roof.

Jochebed, propped against her cushions, sits looking into the fathomless night sky. Since early childhood, she has found comfort in looking at the stars; but tonight, she looks at them with despondency; they offer little comfort with no answers to the questions swirling in her brain.

"Almighty God, are you there? If you really are there, tell me. How can I protect my son?" She begs silently, searching the darkness sprinkled with millions of tiny points of light. "My father says you promised our great ancestor his descendants would be as numerous as the stars in the sky. Will Aaron be in that number? Will my son live to have children of his own?"

Uncertainty is gnawing at her as raw terror is settling into her heart rendering her mind numb and her body exhausted. After some hours she falls into a fitful sleep.

Chapter 9:
Unholy Sacrifice and the Horrific Day of Sorrow

"Thus says the Lord: 'A voice' is heard in Ramah, lamentation, and bitter weeping. Rachel is weeping for her children; she refuses to be comforted for her children because they are not."

Jeremiah 31:15

Mother's instinct brings Jochebed instantly awake. She sits up turning her head from side to side as she attempts to catch a barely audible, rumbling sound. As minutes pass, the distant rumbling sound is growing louder. Straining to determine its source, she rises, careful not to awaken the sleeping family.

The eastern sky is pale with a very faint light signaling the first hint of dawn. All seems quiet in the village. No birds or animals are yet stirring. The rhythmic sounds of breathing tell her everyone is still sleeping peacefully.

Eyes searching in the darkness, the young woman looks toward the south and sees faint lights far in the distance toward the Egyptian city. Suddenly it occurs to her the sounds are the rhythm of horses' hooves and chariots' wheels pounding a hard, rocky road. Turning her ear first in one direction then the other, she strains to pinpoint the location of the horses. An army is approaching fast from the city! Panic swells her chest as if it will explode.

"It is the horses! This is it! Aaron! They are coming for Aaron!"

Grabbing a rough linen robe, she rushes down the stairs to the gate and strains to open it. Fighting the panic, she dashes back up to the roof.

Groping in the darkness, her hands find a wool coverlet that she wraps around Aaron as she gently lifts the sleeping child to her shoulder. Carefully descending the stairs, she carries him to the courtyard.

"I must run! But where? Where do I go? There is nowhere in the village to hide. I must get Aaron away from the red paint on the gate! Run! Run! Run!" All she can think is "Run!" Heaving the gate open, she dashes away from her house in confusion.

"Where will I go? Where will I go?" Cold sweat runs down her face. The hair on her neck stands up; fighting back the urge to cry out, she sprints past the houses as fast as she can run, carrying her child toward the far edge of the village. She holds Aaron's head tightly against her shoulder.

She has gone some distance when the dark form of the weaving shed looms against the pale sky. Quickly she races into the welcome shelter of the shed. The familiar smell of drying reeds and the sight of tools and supplies so ready for a day's work temporarily calms her panic.

Exhausted, breathing heavily, she sinks to the dirt floor with Aaron on her lap. Leaning against a large stack of newly-completed baskets, she rolls her head back against the baskets and looks up at the reed ceiling trying to collect her thoughts.

"Mama! Want Milk! Want milk! Mama!" Aaron whimpers pulling at her robe.

Her heart sinks. He is hungry and ready to nurse. He will soon be crying loudly if he does not nurse soon. Near panic, she strokes his hair to calm him. "There, there, baby, it's all right. Shhh, Shhh, Shhh. Hush! Hush! Don't cry!" she pants.

The sky is growing lighter. Time is draining away. The sounds of chariots and horses are getting louder. There is not enough time to satisfy his hunger. Where can she hide a hungry, crying child?

Frantically, she begs, "O Great and Mighty God, where are you? Help me! Help! Help me! Please don't let them take him from me!"

Her skin is cold and clammy despite the exhausting run; her body is trembling uncontrollably. Suddenly, she jumps as if from an electric shock. Something prickly is crawling on her neck. A scarab beetle with its tiny spiky feet makes its way down her neck. The feeling is like needles pricking on her sensitive skin.

"Ughh," she utters, stifling a scream. "Go away, leave me alone, Khepri! You are watching me even here! How did you find me? Go back to rolling your dung ball!"

A deft flick of her hand sends the yellow beetle flying to the dusty floor. For a moment the beetle rests in the dust; then the little insect spreads its iridescent wings and flies up to her face. It buzzes around her eyes as if to scold her for the rude tumble to the ground.

Aaron stops fretting. Laughing his baby laugh, he points toward the beetle. The beetle circles his head several times and then flies away.

Jochebed stares at the ground where the beetle had been. In the dim light she can see imprinted in the dust the distinct double spiral path where two beetles rolled their ball of sheep dung containing their precious eggs to its place of burial in the ground. A simple plan forms in her head.

"Aaron, look let's play that you are going to be a baby beetle! You will be like that yellow beetle. You will go into your nest, and when you come out, you will fly away like the beetle. Flying will be fun."

As Aaron looks at her curiously, she uses a reed cutter to rip three long strips of cloth from her robe. Spreading Aaron's blanket on the ground, she says firmly, "Lie on your blanket. I will put you in your little nest."

Gently she places him diagonally across the blanket, drawing the lower corner over his feet, and the two side corners across his chest; she starts to bind him tightly in the blanket so he cannot move. Kicking the coverlets away and vigorously waving his hands, Aaron starts to cry.

"No! No! No!! Mama, want milk! Want milk!" he whines wagging his head from side to side.

Terror wells up in her stomach and spills out in her voice. "Stop it! Be still! Hush! Now!"

Her voice cracks with panic as she spits out the words. "If you cry, the demons will eat you! You must be very brave!"

The boy scrutinizes his mother. He has never seen her like this. Her pale face, wide eyes, and strange cracking voice let him know she is not playing a game. His eyes widen in fear; he chokes back cries as tears well up and stream down his little cheeks, and he becomes very still. He dares not object.

Jochebed hurries to bind him in a tight bundle. It breaks her heart to see the look on his face. She longs to hug him and whisk him away to a beautiful, safe place far away from the danger, terror, and ugliness. It frightens him to have his hands and feet bound so tightly and have a cover over his face. She hates to frighten him, but he has no chance of survival without a secure hiding place.

The eastern horizon is glowing pink and lavender with light from the rising sun. Sounds of chariots entering the village from the west road pound her brain. Horsemen are coming around the village from the east. Fear overcomes pity. Quickly she secures the blanket around his body with the two strips from her robe. He cannot move his arms or legs. Pulling the upper corner of the blanket over his face, she ties the third strip over his mouth. He cannot make a cry.

Placing the precious little mummy in a large grain basket, she whispers quietly as she closes the lid, "Now you are going into your nest. Do not make a sound! Brave boys do not cry."

Frantically her fingers weave the lid shut with dry reeds. "You will fly like a beetle when you come out! You must be quiet, or you will not fly!" She pushes the basket among others of similar size and shape. Her treasure is perfectly concealed as she piles several more baskets on top of the stack.

"You are in your nest. Soon you will fly like a beetle. Be very, very quiet! Hush! Hush! Hush! I will take you out soon." One last look to be sure all is secure, she crawls toward the door to peer out toward the road. Seeing no one, she dashes from the shed to the shadows of the nearest building, keeping to the shadow side of the walls. She runs for her life.

The morning is erupting in chaos, as people are awakened by the terror invading their quiet village. Their screams and shouts pierce the crisp air; yells, clamors and sounds of fighting are breaking out everywhere. Ahead she can hear neighing horses, chariot wheels rattling on the stony ground, and shouts of charioteers. Piercing cries of terrified women and children too horrible to imagine send shocks through her body.

Her flying foot hits a loose stone. A flash of sharp pain shoots through her leg as her ankle twists, hurling her to the hard earth. Her hands hit the ground first and then gave way under the force of the fall. Her face slams against a sharp stone protruding from the side of the path. She lies motionless in the dust as minutes pass until throbbing pain brings her back to consciousness. Slowly she pulls herself to a sitting position. Blood from a nasty gash on her cheek forms scarlet rivers through caked dirt as it runs down her face and onto her robe. With bleeding fingers stiff from shock, she tries to brush away the dirt but succeeds only in smearing more blood on her torn, dirty robe.

Two chariots appear. "Woah! Woah!" With a roar, the commander orders the chariots to stop. Until this moment, Jochebed has controlled her panic. The sight of two heavily-armed men approaching, the noise of snorting horses wildly thrashing their hooves so near her, and the smell of the sweaty beasts envelops her. She starts to moan helplessly with violent trembling.

The men loom over her. One of them stoops down and grabs her shoulders roughly shaking her. "What are you doing here?" he demands. "Where is your baby? Why are you here alone?"

Too terrified to speak, Jochebed rolls her head from side to side and moans. Terror explodes into a panic. She begins screaming wildly out of control.

The chariot commander notes her bloody face, torn, dirty clothes, and emotional condition. "Bring her along. It looks as if they've already dealt with her."

One soldier on each side grabs her arm and drags the screaming woman to the center of the village where the people are herded into a tight group. They shove her into the group of villagers where she falls at Ana's feet.

Four wagons pulled by oxen are waiting at the center of the village to be loaded. Helplessly, the people watch as soldiers approach each house marked with red paint. Entering the houses by force, they come out carrying male infants and toddlers. The children are thrown into the wagons like sacks of flour. Family members and occupants of the marked houses are ordered to join the captive group. Only the elderly, young girls, and disabled are allowed to remain in the houses.

Two soldiers, clubs in hand, approach Caleb's house. Kicking in the gate, they cross the courtyard to the house. Caleb stands at the door with a club and refuses to move. The two soldiers attack him with the clubs. His unconscious body is thrown aside. They kick the door open and search every corner of the house. The terrified women watch helplessly as they smash pottery jars destroying every item. A few minutes later they emerge with Joshua and Ezra. Each soldier carries a struggling child by a foot.

With piercing screams, Tirzah rushes to attack like a hysterical cat. Clawing and biting, she throws herself at the nearest soldier. A sharp blow from a club cracks her skull. She falls in a limp heap; her life ebbs away like the crimson stream flowing from her broken skull. The dark pool on the sand marks her heroic but futile attempt to rescue her precious sons. The children dangle from the soldiers' hands like rag dolls. They are thrown into the wagon onto a pile of writhing, bleeding little bodies.

Jeering, dancing, chanting, clapping priests surround the wagons, celebrating each time a child is tossed into the wagon. The noise of the wild celebrations drowns out the children's agonizing screams. When the search of the entire village is complete the wagons move forward to the head of a column.

Chariots lead the way. The people are forced to follow the wagons as armed horsemen lash out with whips and clubs shouting for the people to keep quiet and keep moving. Those who hesitate are lashed with whips, kicked, and beaten unmercifully.

The column of captives is forced to march up a steep path on the side of a hill. The crowd of captives halt at the summit. From this vantage point, there is a clear view of the river some distance below. Men and boys are separated from the women and younger children. They are forced to the edge of the bluff where they can watch the events below.

Women move away from the edge of the cliff, huddling together, they draw some comfort from each other's presence. Some are sobbing, most are ashen-faced and silent. None yet comprehend the full meaning of their plight.

Below, Pharaoh's golden barge is stationed in the center of the river. As the sun's rays strike the brilliant barge, it glistens like the blazing sun, creating a dazzling display of light. The king is an awe-inspiring figure dressed in a white linen robe, red crown, and golden collar inset with shimmering colored jewels with sparkling colors. He sits near the golden altar ready to receive and make sacrifices to the gods of the river.

The sacred shrine brought from its dark sanctuary to make its annual pilgrimage down the river stands on its pedestal as white linen-clad priests dance and sing around the statue, paying loud homage to their god.

Thousands of shouting Egyptians dressed in lavish, feathered costumes and all kinds of exotic dress, line the shores cheering the arrival of their Pharaoh. The celebrating people along with the musicians, dancers, and military form a stamping, shouting throng which raises a cloud of dust and music. Wildly surging emotions whip the revelers to a mob mentality. Gladly they celebrate Pharaoh's commands and claim the horrific sacrifices as their own will.

Built on the edge of the river, the elaborate temple dedicated to the river gods has a special stone dock protruding a short distance into the water. Elevated several feet above the water the dock allows priests to present offerings to the reptile gods without danger of themselves becoming an offering.

The ox wagons pull up to the stone dock. Huge, drab green crocodiles wait patiently. Some are sunning on the beach; others are submerged just below the surface of the murky water. These representatives of Sobek, god of the Nile, have no fear of the barge, the music, or the celebrating people. The noise is a sign food is to be served. Today their banquet will be especially rich. The calm water belies the cruel violence lying beneath its surface.

As the music rises to a shrill crescendo, the priests begin taking the children from the wagons. Amid the screaming, shouting, and cheering, they throw their young victims into the water. Pharaoh is pleased with the sacrifice. It represents to him a major victory over his enemies. He is sure his gods will give him the favor he asks.

When the last child sinks beneath the bloody water, Ra, the mature sun hurls his furious rays into the earth baking everything within his reach. The exhausting heat drains the body of its strength and saps all its energy.

Soldiers dismiss the women and order them to go home. The women trudge slowly, slipping and sliding down the steep path. They are in shock, emotionally, physically, and spiritually drained, they have no more feelings, no more mental power to ponder the magnitude of the sacrifice, and no more energy to dread returning home with empty arms. Their very souls are ripped apart. Even the ability to grieve has been exhausted. Still, they have not yet comprehended the horror of the day. One step at a time they trudge down the dusty path. The stronger support their weak or injured sisters. Children too traumatized to speak trudge with bowed heads behind their mother. All walk along silently staring with unseeing eyes.

When they near the village flocks of black vultures are already gathering in the streets to feed on the bodies of those who perished in the massacre. Swarms of green flies add further insult. When the women think they can endure no more, more is required. Summoning their last reserves of strength, they count their dead and dig shallow graves in the sand at the edge of the village to cover each corpse as there is no time or energy to wrap the bodies with linen and spices.

The temperature is still climbing as midday approaches when Ana and

Judith help Jochebed to her house then quickly leave to help bury the dead. As soon as her friends are gone, Jochebed stands and tests her wounded ankle. The pain is excruciating, but the ankle does not appear to be broken. She holds to the wall and tries to walk on it. Wincing from the intense pain with each step, wobbling back and forth to keep her balance, she finds Amram's shepherd's staff; using it to support herself, she can walk very slowly with the help of the staff.

Ankle throbbing, she covers her head with a wrap and hobbles out the door. Bit by painful bit, she makes her way toward the basket shed. Early this morning she covered this road quickly, but now she makes very slow progress having to rest after two or three steps. As she nears the shed anxiety overcomes the throbbing pain. Forgetting her suffering, she hurries into the shed. The baskets are scattered everywhere. Some are overturned, and some are smashed and torn as if there had been a violent struggle in the shed. Blood is on the floor. Drag marks in the dirt indicate a body was dragged from the shed.

"Aaron, Aaron, please be here!" she whispers desperately, as she goes from basket to basket shaking each one trying to find Aaron's cocoon. Despair is welling up in her breast and about to overcome her last bit of strength when she hears a faint sound.

The sound leads her to her prize. The basket with the lid still woven shut is intact. It is moving. Aaron is rocking it with slight movements. Finding a reed cutter, she slices away the reed lacing and opens the lid. Aaron is very tired, soiled, and hungry, but he is alive and unhurt.

She removes him from the basket. Sitting on the floor, she cuts away the strips of cloth to free him. When Aaron sees her face, he draws away and starts to wail. The sight of her bruised and swollen face with the rivulets of dried blood and dirt upset him.

"It is alright, sweet baby. I am your mama. I am here to take you out of your cocoon. You are alive! I am so happy to see you."

Hugging him to her breast, she is overcome with joy and starts to cry. "You are here! You are here! I can't believe you really are here! Thank you,

Great God, Thank You!"

Aaron's joy in seeing his mother overcomes his fear. "Don't cry, Mama, don't cry. I fly? I fly now?" Aaron asks somewhat dazed.

She laughs and laughs as she hugs him again and again. "What a miracle! You are such a miracle!" she cries joyfully.

It has been hours since he last nursed, and her breasts are swollen and painful. Gritting her teeth against the sharp pain that shoots through her breast as Aaron tugs on it, she momentarily forgets the horror of the day allowing the milk to flow. The tingling feeling of the flowing milk gives her comfort. The beloved smell of her child's hair, the sight of his curled hands while he nurses, and his long eyelashes against his face all bring her a peaceful feeling. Her fingers softly trace Aaron's small face. She strokes the soft skin of his cheek. Her brain records every detail. She focuses on the child to regain her sanity.

Her thoughts drift back to the horror of the day. A low moan escapes her lips as she imagines his small body being thrown into the river to the waiting crocodiles. She sees his blood dripping from the awful jaws, the tiny, limp body cast aside, floating briefly and then sinking into the mud. New waves of panic sweep over her. She feels faint, and her stomach aches. The injuries, forgotten momentarily, throb with intense pain. The unspeakable horror returns to haunt her making her tremble. She will relive this nightmare many, many times.

Suddenly a sharp pain in her breast abruptly interrupts the young mother's thoughts. Aaron is tugging hard on her breast. The milk stopped flowing. The hungry child cries out in frustration. "Milk. Want milk!" he whines.

"We need to go home now; there is no more milk." Aaron looks at her intently, studying her strange appearance. He knows she has changed. He has changed as well. Everything has changed. He does not argue. Arising with the help of the staff she hobbles to the road. Aaron walks slowly beside her with her wrap over his head covering his body. Slowly they make their way home.

The village is still. No one is on the streets. Sounds of bitter weeping and mourning are coming from every house. Grief, like a heavy blanket of despondency, settles over the village. The jarring realization of the day's events is starting to take a cruel effect as the dead are laid to rest. Sorrow is in every courtyard and every corner of each house permeating every facet of life.

Jochebed arrives at her gate by midafternoon. She calls to Mahala to open the gate.

"Mama! Mama! You didn't die! You are here!" Miriam runs to the gate. Mahala is coming behind her. Miriam grabs her mother and almost knocks her to the ground. Jochebed stoops painfully but joyfully hugs Miriam clinging to her for a long moment. Seeing Aaron, the little girl rejoices by clapping her hands and twirling around, dancing in circles. "I have my brother, my brother! I still have a brother!"

Mahala, eyes red and face swollen from weeping, grasps Aaron, pulls him tightly to her breast, and weeps loudly with long-raking sobs.

"It's a miracle! It can only be a miracle from the Almighty!" she gasps through her sobs.

Chapter 10:
The Prophecy and a Message from the Starry Sky

"Rescue me, O my God, from the hand of the wicked, from the grasp of the unjust and cruel man. For thou, O Lord, art my hope, my trust,"

Psalms 71:4-5

    The heavy hand of despair grips the people as they attempt to resume their daily chores. Many go about in grim silence staring with unseeing eyes as if in a trance. Few have the will to protest when the Egyptians announce harder work quotas and increased taxes. Protesting seems futile. No one has regained the strength to challenge the taskmaster's power.

    In former days, Kohath would have called a meeting days earlier, but illness has kept him confined until late afternoon on the 25th day after the Terrible Day of Slaughter. The Levite families file to their meeting place under the palms. Silently, each family leader takes the prescribed place according to rank. Family leaders stand closest to the rock ledge where Kohath will sit to make his speech. Secondary leaders assemble behind the family heads according to their rank. Women and children huddle under the palm trees on the outside of a wide semi-circle. Jochebed sits with Judith and Ana. The women group close together waiting to hear if Kohath will offer them any comfort. The congregation waits silently for their leader to speak.

    The Place of the Palms is the accustomed meeting place for tribal gatherings. At the base of steep cliffs, a stream of water provides a place where palms grow and supplies a shaded grassy area for the people to assemble. The cliffs form a natural backdrop for a stone stage.

Two men carry the old chief on a stretcher made of cowhide and wooden poles. They laboriously climb the rocky path until they reach the high stone seat. Placing a ram skin on the stone, they help the old one off the stretcher. With shaky, faltering steps he moves to the stone seat and positions himself for his discourse.

A young man posts the tribal standard. Amram sits at his right hand to signify he is in line as successor to the leader of the tribe. The old one looks down at his congregation from his throne on the ledge. His dim vision prevents him from recognizing anyone. He knows this will likely be his last speech to his people.

Kohath appears more tired and even older than on the previous occasion when he made a public appearance. His red lower eyelids sag on his cheeks. His voice is very weak. He lifts his trembling hand as a signal he is ready to address the tribe. His voice comes out in a coarse whisper. The young man who has been chosen to assist him stands at his side to call out his words so all can hear.

"My dear children, children of our great Father Levi! Levi the son of Jacob, son of Isaac, son of the Most Faithful Abraham, our hearts are very heavy. Your backs are bleeding from the taskmaster's whip! Bruises cover your body. Burdens are growing heavier and heavier. Bitterness and sorrow fill our lives. We ache and find no comfort. Our children are sacrificed as offerings to wicked gods."

Screams and moans erupt from the women. Mournful wrenching sobs, wailing, and cries of deep loss rise to the heavens. The spokesman raises both hands and calls for quiet. After some minutes, the wailing lessens to a muffled sobbing. Pausing for a long minute, Kohath speaks again.

"Long, long ago, one evening such as this, as the sun was setting, our father, Abraham, fell into a deep sleep. The Almighty God said to him, your descendants will be slaves in a foreign land, and they will be oppressed for four hundred years."

He pauses to collect his thoughts.

"Just as the Almighty said, we are wrongly oppressed as slaves. But the

Lord said to our father, 'Your people will come out from under the slavery with great possessions.' On that same day, the Lord God of Heaven and Earth made a solemn contract with our Father saying, 'I have given you this land from the river of Egypt to the great river Euphrates.' The contract was sealed with sacrifices and blood. It cannot and will not be broken. The beautiful land of Canaan where our father lived is ours. One day you will possess it. The Lord said that our family has been chosen to carry the child of Eve who will bless all people by triumphing over wickedness. This is the reason the land will be ours."

He makes a triumphant gesture with his hands and waits until the young man has finished calling out his words.

"These days are very dark, but the dawn will break. This wicked nation of people who oppress us will be punished. Our God has not deserted us. Many have already departed this life. We mourn them. They sleep in a place of peace where soon I too will go to sleep with them. But some of you here today may see this salvation."

Suddenly his eyes take on a new light. His voice becomes more resolute. New life seems to flow into the trembling, old body.

"Hear this, all you Levites!" he shouts. "Do not fear or let your hearts be discouraged!"

The young spokesman stunned, forgets to speak. In a loud voice, Kohath continues.

"The wicked gods of Egypt will not defeat us! Our time here is almost finished! You will go back to our homeland! Your flocks and herds will graze in peace. Our God, like a good shepherd, will lead you back to our promised land as a shepherd leads his flock. Take heart and have faith. Hold onto the hand of the Almighty. His promise is unbreakable. You will see it!"

His frail white hands rise heavenward as if stretching to grasp an unseen hand reaching down to take hold of him from on high. For a moment his hands flutter in the air as if they are unable to grasp the extended hand. Like wounded doves, his quivering hands fall back to his lap. Exhausted, he slumps forward; his beard falls back on his breast. He is unable to speak any longer.

The congregation stares at the old man in dumb disbelief. Darkening shadows contrast sharply with the pale face, snow-white hair and beard, making the fragile form glow like a ghost against the rocky wall. There is silence. The only sound is the gentle rustle of the palm fronds swaying in the breeze. The words hang in the air. Within a few minutes, the old one's words are carried away by the wind.

When Amram stands, raising his hands, and shouts to gain the attention of the crowd, the people have already turned away to gather in small groups and talk among themselves in grumbling low tones.

"Crazy old fool! He doesn't have to make bricks in the hot sun. He doesn't have to feel the whips! He would be singing a different song if he had to march out to work every morning for this stinking, God-forsaken, crocodile-worshiping, Egyptian monsters. Where is this Almighty God when we need Him?" Asher bitterly spits at the ground.

"Does this look like I'm going to march out of here in victory?" Rueben points with his right thumb to a hideous, swollen, infected wound that runs from his left eye down his face and onto his shoulder. His limp left arm is supported in a sling.

"This is what I got for trying to defend my son. Now he is dead. What do I have to hope for? I wish to die here and soon. I may as well be dead. I have nothing left but more days working for these cursed devils."

Asher curses bitterly, "I hear you. What good is a promise without our sons? If we have more sons, these blood-sucking monsters will just take them too. This talk about a land of freedom is a joke. I will believe it when I see the Great River running red with my taskmaster's blood and the crocks eating at old Pharaoh's carcass."

As despair settles over the camp like a wet, polluting fog, the families slowly rise and drift back to their houses. In silence, Jochebed follows Judith and Ana as they make their path back to the village.

"Do you really believe our father Abraham made a contract with the

Almighty God?" asks Ana. "I have always believed so but now it seems no one else is sure of it. Where is this mighty God now? No one has seen Him lately. Every time we think things can't get worse, something else even more terrible happens. Working hard and paying taxes is hard, but we are strong, and we can take it. Losing our people is something we cannot suffer very long. I can't forget the sight of Tirzah's cruel death. And her children she loved so much were thrown away like rubbish in a dung heap. What will happen to the rest of us?"

Judith says, "If there is a God who cares about us, why are we suffering so much? What kind of a God allows all this to happen? How can a God who cares about women and children allow such terrible suffering? The Almighty God must be a wicked god! The Egyptian gods seem to give their people everything they need. The Egyptians are happy, but we are miserable. So many children died! I am wondering if this God is even strong enough to save us." Resentment rings from her speech.

Jochebed whispers softly, "I believe the Great God helped me to save Aaron."

"Oh! Is that right?" Judith retorts. "Then why did the Great God save your son but not save so many others? My sister lost two sons, and my brother lost his first and only child! So why did the Great God favor you? You say you just happened to think about the grain baskets and hide him. How did you know to go to the weaving shed? Maybe Amram made a deal with the Egyptians to save your son in exchange for information about other people's children. Maybe this is the reason your son is not dead like so many others." Judith spits out the words bitterly.

"That's not true," Jochebed says through tears, smitten by the stinging accusation. She trudges along in silence staring out into the distance all the way home. More tears stream down her face. When she reaches her house, she leaves her companions at the gate without a word and ascends the stairs to the roof where Mahala is with Miriam and Aaron. The children are sleeping soundly.

Mahala rouses from her sleep. "Oh. Where are Amram and Sarah? Will they be home soon?"

"I don't know. It went very badly," Jochebed's voice is breaking. "The men seem on the point of rebellion against my father." The distraught young woman sits on a lambskin. She draws a trembling breath and breaks into weeping.

"Oh, Child, tell me about it. What happened?" Mahala comes near and puts her arm around her daughter-in-law.

The young woman weeps harder. "Father said our God will lead our people to victory as a shepherd leads a flock of sheep. He said the Lord would keep His promises," she gasps between sobs.

"He has said this for many years. But this time the men made fun of him and mocked him. They even called him an old fool! I do not know what is happening. If what my father says is true, why is there so much suffering? Some are saying that our God must be wicked to allow the children to die. Why did the children die? I can't help thinking of dear Tirzah. I miss her so much. How could a kind God let her die? Her sons and husband are dead too. They are gone! Even my friends are saying there is no God. They are accusing us of making deals with the Egyptians. What will happen to us? Is there any hope?" She weeps from a heart too heavy with grief and pain.

Mahala pulls the young woman closer to her breast and holds her until the sobbing subsides.

"Child, I cannot tell you everything will be all right. We have seen too much suffering. We lost many people, yet I do know the Almighty cares for his people. We cannot see all His reasons why He allows things to happen as they do." She is silent for a long moment.

When she speaks, her words come slowly. "What is this you are sitting on?" she asks stroking the soft wool on the lambskin.

Jochebed digs her fingers into the plush wool. "What? Do you mean this lambskin?"

"Yes. You said it. It was a lamb's skin. A shepherd cares for his sheep.

He leads them to food and water, and he protects them from all danger. Sometimes he even risks his own life for his sheep, but from time to time he takes some of the lambs and slaughters them. The shepherd decides which sheep will live and which will die. The ones that are chosen to die are like sacrifices for the other sheep because they are allowed to live longer. In the end, all the sheep die for the shepherd. Is the shepherd wicked because he kills the sheep?"

"No. Shepherds are not wicked. But we understand why the shepherd must take the lambs and kill the sheep. We can see all this." She thinks for a moment. "But if a sheep could know her lambs may die, will she still follow the shepherd?"

Again, Mahala answers after a long pause.

"Yes. She will follow the shepherd because without the shepherd she cannot live. She gives her all to the shepherd because he is her only hope to live."

Aaron stirs restlessly, making whimpering sounds as if he will wake. Immediately Mahala is at his side patting his back and crooning a soft lullaby to soothe him back to sleep. Covering herself and the boy with a goat skin blanket to shield him from the cool wind she curls up beside him. He is quiet again. She pats him until they both drift into a sound sleep.

Jochebed sits propped on leather cushions staring up into the moonless, starry sky. The stars appear to surround her, so near she can reach out and touch them. The sight is familiar and comforting like long-time friends who come to visit at night bringing good news. Her eyes search the constellations in the myriads of blinking stars. Stretching from the eastern horizon overhead into the Milky Way and across the western sky. There are so many, many thousands of twinkling points of light; the breathtaking sight makes her dizzy as she tries to take in the vastness. A shooting star streaks across the sky and burns out. There are no less lights than before. The heavens are not diminished by the loss of the shooting stars.

"Our ancient fathers said you speak with silent voices that tell a story of triumph over the enemy," she muses softly. "Almighty God, you pointed to the stars when You promised to give our father Abraham, many descendants. Our people will be as numerous as the stars, you said. The stars were there for Abraham to see. They are here for me to see as well. Almighty God, are you speaking to me through these stars?"

The stars seem to become brighter. Some seem to move.

"Are you speaking to me as you did to our ancestors? Do I hear your silent voices? From our people, the child of Eve will come to defeat the enemy. Are you saying this promise is as enduring as the stars and cannot be broken?"

"So then, no enemy can defeat us. Pharaoh cannot silence the stars by making life hard for us. Nothing on this earth can take away the stars or God's promise. Nothing on earth will defeat us because God promised it. Not even our own people's unbelief will dim one of these tiny lights. Stars are unmovable by anything on Earth. Like Almighty God's word, stars are fixed for all time. Even though right now things are bad for us, our suffering does not mean God has forgotten his promise."

As she ponders these thoughts the stars seem to sing joyfully as if an invisible master conductor is directing them with perfect harmony in a glorious chorus of praise to their Creator.

"You are singing for me! Do you see me, Almighty God? I feel you must be looking at me. You are showing me a message with these stars!" she exclaims softly.

"Now I understand! These stars are singing a song of victory. One day there will be victory. Your promise is as sure as these stars. Somehow, some way You will save our people. I want my children to sing in your chorus of stars. I want to sing there too!"

An awesome realization of the Great, Everlasting Creator leaves her silently staring into the sky until the first rays of dawn breaking over the horizon wipe the stars away.

Chapter 11:
A Divine Blessing and Resolute Determination

"For my thoughts are not your thoughts, nor are my ways, your ways, says the Lord. For as the heavens are higher than the earth, so are my ways higher than your ways, and my thoughts than your thoughts."

Isaiah 55:8-9

Kohath has not left his house since the meeting at the Place of the Palms. Most of his time has been spent on his bed of stacked sheep skins. He has little energy and wants to see no one except Hogla and his most trusted family members. Since his last appearance, he has spoken only when his physical needs require speech.

When Amram learned of his grandfather's poor state of health, he came immediately to find the old leader on his bed leaning against a heap of woolen blankets. He holds the old man's fragile hand as he kneels beside the bed.

"Grandfather, I am so sorry to see you so sick. There is usually a light in your eyes, and you have much to say. What pain is making you feel so bad? We are all worried about you."

"I am sick at heart, my son. I am very sick at heart. I should have passed the leadership of the Levite Tribe to you at the time of your wedding. Anointing you would have been the right thing to do. You could have been leading the people and keeping the tribe together. But I have been a selfish old man who refused to give up his power and control. Even when I knew I was too old and weak to lead the people."

Tears stream down his face. He sniffs forcefully through his nose as he tries to wipe the tears away with rigid, curled fingers.

"The people were right to call me a crazy, old fool. That is what an old man becomes when he thinks only of himself. Believing I could lead this great tribe was foolish when I couldn't walk to my seat under the sycamore tree without a woman's help."

He blows his nose and wipes his face with a rag.

"I may have destroyed all that I have worked so many years to accomplish. My foolishness has diminished the people's trust in our God and caused some people to turn toward Egyptian idols for comfort. Others have settled into hopelessness. Please forgive me, son. Your job will be harder because of my grave errors. All I want now is to see you successful and the people led back to the path of God."

Amram attempts to comfort his grandfather. "No, Grandfather, you are not an old fool. You have been a great leader. The times are hard, and the people are discouraged but all is not lost. We must work together to regain their trust and rebuild their lives and their faith in our God,"

"No son," Kohath says, "Do not say 'we will build the tribe together.' It is you who will rebuild the tribe. My time has passed. You are to take the leadership immediately. Your time has come. I must see you anointed leader before I die. Please do this for your God, for your people, and for me, your foolish, old grandfather."

"I will arrange the anointing, Grandfather. Please do not say anything to anyone. Some of my friends will be here soon. They will stay with you until I return. We will do this today."

On leaving the house, Amram pauses at the gate where Benaiah waits. He tells his friend that Kohath is ready for the anointing to happen immediately.

"Are you feeling a heavy weight pressing on your shoulders?" Benaiah asks.

A serious look crosses Amram's face. "I have been thinking about this since Grandfather said he would appoint me as leader. I knew this day was coming, but I do not know if I am ready for it. Even though I have some plans, the reality of the responsibility is just now starting to sink in."

He waves toward the mud brick houses that are scattered randomly like child's blocks tossed on the playroom floor. The structures are connected by worn footpaths that indicate the resident's interaction with each other.

"All these people are going to be looking to me for guidance. Some will think I am the Almighty who can work miracles; others will curse me saying I am an inept, lying, cheating criminal who stole the leadership from his weak old grandfather."

Benaiah says grinning, "Yep. Those last ones you mentioned would be your uncles. What will you do about them?"

As the heavy thoughts start to sink into Amram's head, he says with a worried look, "I can't stop their mouths or their planning to depose me. That is the reason I need you to help me. A confrontation with them will come. I do not know how or when. I just want to be ready for it. I know this confrontation could be very dangerous."

Eager to declare his loyalty, Benaiah says with confidence, "We have been friends ever since we were small boys running naked in the courtyard. We have done many things together. You are like my brother. I will do anything you want me to do. I am not afraid if you are with me."

A smile of relief passes over Amram's face, "That is all I need to know. Will you call the men together? Send three of them here to wait at this house with Grandfather. Tell them to make sure they bring their weapons. Then go to the village square and sound the shofar. Call an assembly. Announce that a new leader is to be anointed at once. March the procession to this house where we will be waiting. Grandfather will anoint me as leader. He will place the leader's robe and medallion on me. He will make it clear for all to see and hear. All will see for themselves who will be chosen as their leader."

A broad smile lights Benaiah's ruddy face. He throws his head back and laughs loudly.

"Ha! Ha! Ha! This may be a lot of fun! Those three reprobates who are called your uncles will be hopping mad! They will be so hot we may light our torches with their heads at the celebration tonight!"

Laughing loudly, they slap each other on the shoulder, obviously enjoying the imagery.

Still laughing, Benaiah says, "Everyone knows they are hoping your grandfather will pass before he anoints you! They will not have time to plan a way to stop the anointing. It will be too late for them to come whining, bawling, and trying to browbeat your grandfather into changing his mind. This is good!"

"You got it, man!" Amram shouts as the two friends head toward the village center. " That is the plan! We will set up our place of judgment in the village square near the well where it was in the past. This is where the people come every day. We will hear their complaints and concerns. We will talk to them and win them to us. Together with the Almighty, we are going to rebuild this tattered tribe! Maybe the Almighty will give us a sign of his favor. Ben, my friend, we are in this together. You are my man!"

After the work day has ended, Benaiah returns; blowing the shofar and followed by his troop of warriors, they surround Kohath's house. Kohath is sitting in his place of judgment waiting for them. Amram receives the blessing and the appointment as tribal leader.

Hearing the noise, Abahail's three sons rush to the scene with some of their collaborators, but Amram's friends do not allow them to enter the courtyard. The trio slinks away like coyotes that have been outsmarted by their prey. They will wait and watch for another opportunity to make a strike. They are confident a break will open to them soon.

Amram is anointed without interference. He assumes his role as a leader with hopeful anticipation. Although he seems to be enjoying the prospect of elevating the mood of his people and giving them some hope, his time with his family has been shortened and his burdens heavier.

When Jochebed feels the familiar wiggling in her belly, she hesitates to discuss it with her husband because she does not want to trouble him with more problems. Just a few weeks ago, she realized another child was growing inside her. She waits weeks before telling her husband, but her mother-in-law is first to know.

"I wish I could feel happy about this baby," she says to Mahala as they are preparing the daily bread.

"Remember when we celebrated Aaron's birth? Amram was so happy to have a son he stayed up all night celebrating with his friends. What if this baby is a boy? What will we do? Will it be possible to keep this pregnancy a secret?"

A shadow of fear crosses her face.

"Amram says Abahail's sons are talking more and more to the Egyptian taskmasters. Could they already suspect I am carrying a child?"

Mahala looks up from the stone plate where she is grinding the flour.

"We have been diligent to keep your pregnancy a secret because we must do it. Abahail's sons may be wondering if you are carrying a baby, but they do not know that for sure. We will use every way we know to keep it from them. This means we must start to plan immediately. Everything thing must be planned carefully if we hope to hide the birth from them."

Mahala brushes the flour into a shallow bowl and then stirs oil into the flour to make the dough.

"We can trust Sarah, but no one else must know about it, not even your father or your mother. You will have to wear a larger tunic when you go to the fields. Keep Aaron nursing, or your breasts will swell and let others know your secret. You must not go out to the garden or to the river with anyone except Sarah. When the time for the birth arrives, we will say you are sick and cannot go to work for a few days. We must prepare for the baby to be a boy but hope it is a girl."

Jochebed fans the fire preparing to cook the bread.

"Amram will be punished severely like some of the other fathers if we try to hide the birth. They do not wait for the festival now; they come to take the child as soon as they know about the birth of a boy. There is no place to hide. A newborn will not survive many hours in a grain basket or any other hiding place, even if we could hide him. I do not know what to do. I will do anything to save my child. It is going to be very hard to hide a child until he is three years old."

Mahala takes a lump of dough and pats it into a loaf.

"You will think of a way. Have faith. Pray that the Almighty will help you save this child. As Aaron was spared, so must this one be spared. We will do all we can to help you. That is all we can do. "

The months pass too quickly. As the pregnancy nears its term, preparations made in secret are completed. Supplies are smuggled into the house and hidden in large jars with fitted lids that stand in the corners of the room. Herbs to be used in the birth process are hung from the ceiling. The birth bricks are hidden under the clothes and blankets. All must be close at hand when the need for them arrives.

Late one day while Jochebed is working in the field, she feels the first squeezing sensations in her belly. For the next few hours, she monitors the sensations as they grow stronger. When she returns home, she lets her family know this may be the night the baby arrives. After the evening meal, she goes to the roof with the family until midnight. A couple of hours after midnight, she wakes Sarah and Mahala.

"The pains are getting stronger now. I think it is time to go down to the birth bricks," Jochebed whispers to prevent waking the children.

The women slip down to the darkness of the room where the birth will occur. Coals prepared earlier during the afternoon were stored in a clay jar waiting to be used to light the small oil lamps with lighters made from twisted straw. A glimmering glow from the two small lamps set in niches in the wall give subdued light to the room.

The black goat skin that Amram hung on a rolled shaft above the window is let down to cover the window. A similar black goat skin blanket is hung across the door. Sarah slips out to view the house to make sure not even a flicker of light can seep through the windows or door to give even a hint of their secret activity inside.

Mahala goes to the back of the courtyard where a bed of coals keeps a pot of water hot. The water will be used to prepare herbs for lessening pain.

Jochebed walks into the dimness of the room to relieve her tension, Sarah speaks encouraging words in low whispers.

"Keep your voice low. Take this stick and bite it when the pain becomes too hard. Biting it will help you to prevent loud moaning. We don't want anyone to hear your labor now," Sarah admonishes.

As the night progresses, the contractions continue to intensify. The birth bricks are placed at the ready as transition labor begins. As dawn approaches the pink dawning light spreads above the mountains. Mahala goes to the roof.

"Amram, come down. We need help. The baby is ready to come. We need you to help support Jochebed while she pushes. She is becoming tired. This has been a long difficult labor," Mahala whisper.

Amram descends the stairs where he finds his wife squatting on the birthing bricks. Sarah is having difficulty supporting her. Jochebed is in hard labor. Her teeth are clamped tight on the stick, but moans escape from her mouth. Amram lifts her arms and places them on his shoulders.

"Push against me. I can hold you up," he says as he claps his hands behind her back. His arms encircle her. He squats down and faces her.

Jochebed rouses herself and clenches her fingers onto the hard flesh of her husband's muscular shoulders. His strength seems to encourage her to renewed efforts to carry on. She rises higher on the bricks, and then with feet wide apart pushes down on the baby with all her might. The baby descends into the birth canal and the head crowns. Her fingernails dig red marks in Amram's shoulders. Once again, she pushes with all her strength. She feels her body let go to allow the child to be released. When the infant slides out, Mahala catches the small, slick body and holds it in triumph. The child emits a lusty cry.

"We did it! The baby is breathing! It is a strong child! It is a boy!" Mahala says trying to keep her voice as soft as possible. She places her finger gently over the baby's tiny mouth to stifle any more cries.

Sarah lifts the goat skin from the window to let in light. After Mahala has thoroughly examined the baby and is satisfied the child is healthy, she cuts the umbilical cord and wipes him off with a soft cloth.

Amram lifts his exhausted wife to a blanket then reaches for the infant. He cradles the child in his two big, rough paws, studying the small face. He speaks to his tiny, newly-arrived son.

"You are a fine, strong boy. A few years ago, I would have been yelling for joy to know I have two big boys. Now I do not know whether to be happy or sad. You have come into a world of trouble and hardship. I wish it were better, but it is all we have. You will have to share our troublesome and sorrowful lives. If I could change it, I would, but right now I can't do anything about it. There is one good thing you do have. You have a good mother. Son, meet your mother."

Jochebed rolls over on her side. She supports herself on her elbow as she watches her husband and new son.

"See here is our little man who caused you so much pain." Amram's calloused, work-worn hands raise the delicate babe in front of the window so Jochebed can see him clearly. The dawn light has grown brighter.

The tiny person looks at his mother with his intense, bright eyes. He appears as if he has just come from a long distance to bring her some important message. He is more beautiful than any child she has seen. Looking into his eyes is like looking at the vastness of the stars. He encompasses the past, the present, and the future all at the same time. For a moment mother and child contemplate each other.

Suddenly brilliant rays from the rising sun send a shaft of light through the high east window striking the newborn baby, blessing him in dazzling radiance. He squints his little eyes against the brightness and twists his face against the brilliance.

"Look at that! Look at him! What does this mean?" Sarah gasps astonished. "Oh, my God! Oh, my God!"

Awe-struck, Mahala sinks on her knees to the floor. "He is a holy person! What are we going to do! What will we do with him?! This is too much! The Almighty has sent us a holy person! Oh, Almighty God, what do you want us to do now? You have put even more trouble on us!" She covers her face with her hands.

Amram finds his voice. "No. He is not trouble for us. He is a promise from God. He will protect our family and all his people. He is the son of our Mother Eve. He will save us. He is our hope and our joy. The Almighty God will help us save him and our people."

Jochebed contemplates her infant son. His doll-like body supported in his father's big, rough hands appears so fragile and helpless, yet he is fully present. A fire of determination flames deep within the young mother. At this moment she knows she will risk everything for him. Whatever she must do to save him from Pharaoh's wrath she will do. She knows she will pay any price to accomplish this task.

Some people in ancient nations believed if the rays from the rising sun shown on a newborn baby shortly after its birth, the child was anointed by God for a special mission. The sun's rays were considered a distinct blessing from God.

Chapter 12:
The Dismal Princess and an Overheard Conversation

"For I am God, and there is no other; I am God there is none like me. Declaring the end from the beginning, and from ancient times things that are yet to be done. Saying 'My council shall stand.'"

Isaiah 46:9-10

Women no longer gather at the weaving shed to talk together as before. The accustomed gathering places are vacant. Grandmothers and all others who are caretakers of children keep the young ones out of sight. No one is sure who can be trusted. Pharaoh's orders that all male children are to be taken as soon as they are born has brought about suspicion, fear, and isolation in the usually vibrant village.

Women of childbearing age deem it essential that no one know for sure who is carrying a child: therefore, they, also remain out of sight as much as possible. When working in the fields, all wear extra-large tunics so pregnancy is not easy to detect. Their head wraps are pulled low over their eyebrows and high around the neck to hide their identity even from fellow Hebrews. Suspicion and fear of neighbors increase as the collective focus is on protecting their families.

Sarah and Jochebed must get more reeds for the indispensable basket-making. The selling and trading of the baskets are necessary to gain money to maintain the family. Their supplies of reeds are low. More reeds must be obtained while most of the Egyptians are busy preparing for another feast day.

To avoid any trouble with the men working along the river, the women rise very early before dawn and travel by the light of the setting moon to find a new place to cut reeds. They know they are taking a gamble. In the usual places where they work, there is too much risk of meeting familiar people who also may be dangerous. They must go further down the river away from known territory. By the time the sun appears they come to a new place that looks desirable.

A stone cabana stands near the trees a few yards from the edge of the river. Near the entrance of the cabana is a limestone statue of the crocodile god, Sobek. The stones which compose the altar are intricately cut and fitted together with skilled workmanship. An inscription carved on a stone face in front pays homage to one of Egypt's most powerful gods. On top of the altar is a basin where people leave their offerings and gifts.

Jochebed and Sarah survey the scene taking note of all the details of the new location.

"Look at that image of Sobek. It is a man with a crocodile's head. Who would worship that hideous thing? But the bathhouse and the rest are very pretty and luxurious. This must be a bathing place," Jochebed says.

"I do not like that ugly statue of a crocodile man. It is creepy. Just think people leave gifts on that altar. Maybe we should leave now before we get into real trouble," Sarah says.

Jochebed sniffs, "Huh. That ugly piece of rock cannot tell on us. I want to smear it with mud! It can't see or say anything. Why should we fear a deaf and dumb piece of rock?"

Alarmed, Sarah says, "No! you can't do that! They would search until they found who did it and put us in prison or worse! Insulting this rock would only get us in trouble. This represents their powerful god. They worship it."

Jochebed takes a calmer tone, "I know, I know. It was a foolish thing to say. But I am still so angry that they sacrificed our children to this evil god, I want to get some kind of revenge."

Sarah, still cautious, says, "Save your revenge for another time and a different way. I'm not afraid of the slab of rock. I am afraid of the people who put it there and the evil that demands their worship. They expect everyone to honor it as a god. We need to leave this place before anyone sees us."

"This is such a nice place," Jochebed rationalizes her desire to stay and work here. "It is the best place we have found since we have been searching for a place to get basket materials. If we work on the other side of the reeds, we can't see this statue. I do not see any signs that people have been here lately. Besides we have a clear view of the river from both directions, and there are thick bulrushes and low-hanging tree limbs to hide us if we see anyone coming."

"Yes, I like this place very much," Sarah replies, becoming convinced of the desirability of the site, "The water is clear. We can rest near the cool water under those trees. This must be a special place. See, there are plenty of reeds here. This means no one has been cutting any at this place. We will have to be very careful to hide any signs we have been here," she says, scanning the water for any signs of crocodiles.

Satisfied they will work here, Jochebed says, "Let's keep close to the trees in the thick reeds so we will not be seen by anyone who is in a boat. Each of us must be watching every minute. If we see anyone, we can get under the trees quickly. You watch that direction, and I will watch this way. Keep your eyes open every minute."

The women start to work cutting reeds. Jochebed spots a raptor soaring high above them.

"Horus sees everything. He is watching us even as we work in this new place. Is there no place safe from his eyes? He follows us even to this new spot. No one can see us from the river or the shore, but old Horus is in the air watching us all the time. How long will it be before he knows about my son?" She deftly cuts a papyrus stalk with her sharp stone knife. Quickly a pile of reeds starts to grow.

A cargo boat sails silently past. The women squat in the water behind the vegetation to conceal themselves from the men rowing the boat.

"Oh, how I wish we could sail far, far away on a boat! They say boats go to strange lands. Maybe this river will take us to another land so far away Pharaoh will never find us," Sarah muses.

"So do I, but we do not have a boat. Pharaoh does not allow any Israelites to leave here. It would be impossible to leave this place with three young children. How could we feed them? We do not know where to go. A boat will not help us save Little Brother." Jochebed answers.

As Jochebed reaches to grasp a handful of reeds, she is startled by an explosion of feathers bursting out of a thick mass of entwined stalks. With pitiful cries, a bittern skims the water falling, rising, struggling, and falling again as if it has a broken wing. The hawk follows the bird hoping to capture it, but the bittern escapes into a twisted tangle of reeds.

Taken aback by the outburst, Jochebed drops her cutter in the water. "Oh! Oh! That scared me! I thought it was a croc or something worse jumping out to get me! It was just a bird!" she exclaims, putting her hands over her chest to still her thumping heart.

Sarah laughs, "You should have seen yourself. You looked like you were about to be eaten by a demon. We have been working all around this place, and we never saw that bird until you almost touched her. She must have been sitting on her nest all this time."

Jochebed searches the clump of reeds where the bird was hiding. Finally, her eyes fall on a perfectly concealed nest containing two newly-hatched baby birds and two eggs. A tangled mass of grass and sticks hides the little treasure. Only a very diligent predator would be able to detect its presence.

"Horus did not see these little birds. They were right under his eyes, but he never saw them. If you can make a hiding place like this mother bird, you can hide your babies as well," says Sarah.

"You are right, Sarah. That is what I need to do. I need a place right under old Pharaoh's eyes."

The conversation is interrupted when they suddenly spot a slender, brilliantly-colored cedar wood boat fast approaching. Four women are sitting under a fringed canopy in the center of the craft. Two men are at either end using oars to power the vessel. Another man stands at the fore of the boat to watch for activity happening on the river.

"Look! A boat is coming!" Jochebed says with urgency. "They look like people from Pharaoh's house! Before they see us get under this tree! Let's see what they are going to do."

The women wade in the dark shade beneath the branches of a low-hanging tree surrounded by profuse growth of marsh grasses. Sinking in the dark water until it covers their shoulders, they watch as the lightweight boat skims the shoreline. It comes within yards of the women who are concealed by the shaded water and marsh grasses.

Fazel thrusts his oar into the riverbed and uses it to push the bow of the boat onto the shore. He gets out and with the help of his fellow servants, he pulls the craft onto the beech. They scrutinize the area for crocodiles. Finding none, Fazel turns his attention to the women.

Extending his hand to help Queen Nephre disembark he is careful to be sure the queen is safely on land before offering his assistance to Princess Meryt.

The princess daintily steps out onto the soft silt of the beach. The sheer white-pleated linen dress does not hide her gaunt thinness. Like a delicate water nymph, her form appears fragile; her movements and steps are slow, not consistent with a girl her age. The large, dark eyes painted with kohl appear sunken into her pale face. The eyes brim with sadness. The gold jewelry on her gaunt arms and ears glistens in the sun, but her mood is somber. Her skin seems to sag on her face. She looks older than her age.

The men station themselves on the beach in positions where they can keep a close watch for any kind of danger.

Nuti and Titi carrying bathing supplies exit from the craft. Their baskets are filled with scented oils, lotions, and soaps for washing the body and hair. Dry clothing, combs, hair brushes, and towels are packed in linen bags. The servant women carry their supplies to the bathhouse.

Queen Nephre surveys the water and beach. "Our boat ride was so delightful this wonderful morning. Do you agree, dear? It is good to get away from the palace for a while."

Meryt nods in agreement by slightly lowering her chin. Her mouth pulls back very slightly. She sighs with a shrug of her shoulders.

"Isn't this a lovely place, dear? This morning is so beautiful. See the water is clear and sparkling. The trees make it cool. Do you remember when this was your favorite bathing place? You were always so happy when we came here. You called it your magic place. We have not been here in quite a while. A bath at this lovely site should cheer you up. Please. Will you try it and see if it cheers you?"

"Yes, I have always liked this place. I wish I could be as happy as I was when we used to come here often. The water is cool. It will feel good." Meryt has little emotion in her barely audible voice.

"Come, dear. We need to pay homage to our god. He is powerful. Maybe he will decide to help you. Nuti, bring the offerings."

Offerings of date cakes and wine are placed on the altar and the incantations imploring the help of the river god are uttered. "There. Now I feel we are safe. You can feel good here as you bathe," the queen says confidently.

Nuti and Titi prepare the princess for her bath. When she is ready to enter the water Titi helps the girl slowly make her way down the stone stairs.

Meryt dabbles with her toe in the water without enthusiasm. Slowly, little by little, she wades until the water is above her knees. Her fingertips lightly skim the surface making it move in small whirls. She stares off into space as if preoccupied with other concerns. The queen with worried eyes sits on the bench and watches as her daughter gingerly splashes about.

Strolling along the river's edge for a short distance Titi and Nuti pause to chat in the shadow of the tree where Sarah and Jochebed are hiding behind the thick reeds and river grasses.

"She used to be such a happy girl. Now she is the picture of gloom.

She hardly eats or sleeps. Queen is so worried. She is afraid the girl will die from a broken heart. That woman has done everything she knows to do, but nothing can get her daughter out of her depression. She has consulted every soothsayer and tried every magic spell, but nothing works. Ever since her baby died, the poor girl has been depressed. Even the wise men of the court are unable to help her. The only thing the princess can talk about is her lost baby. At night I hear her crying." Titi says sorrowfully.

"It is very sad," Nuti agrees. "Lady Meryt had big dreams. She wanted her son to become the next king of Egypt. Now that hope is gone. The physicians say she will not have children. It is so, so sad. Her rival sisters make fun of her. They laugh because someone else's son will be the next Pharaoh. The princess feels she is a failure. It has been two years since she lost her baby, so I do not think time will heal her. What she needs is a baby to restore her dream and purpose. Only a son can make her happy. If she cannot give birth to a child, she is doomed to a failed life. She will be replaced by one of her rival sisters."

Niti's face takes on a somber look. "If the princess dies, the Queen will die too. She says she cannot face being replaced by another wife whose daughter has a son to succeed Pharaoh."

Nuti draws her lips tight across her teeth. "If this happens, what will happen to us? The next queen will have her own maids. She will send us away. There will be no use for us in the palace. We will have to work hard chores away from the Great House. We will be field workers or worse. This is scaring me. I'm not usually afraid, but I do not know what to do about this."

Titi shudders. "I have thought about this problem many times. It is true. The princess does not seem to be getting better. I am worried about what will happen. I have asked the soothsayers what to do, and they do not give me the answers I want to hear. One even told me I would not stay in the palace. I am having scary dreams. Terrible things may happen to us."

"Come along, girls," Nephre calls to the maids.

Nuti and Titi come to help Meryt wash her hair. In the bath house the servant women anoint the princess with oil and perfume and help her dress in dry clothing. She is ready to return to the palace.

"Did you have a pleasant bath? You look refreshed after a cool dip. Do you feel better, Dear?"

"I do feel a little better. The water was nice." Meryt relies in a low mumble.

"Oh, excellent! I am so glad to hear you say that. This will become your favorite bathing site again. You are going to be healed! I feel magic is here! The gods who inhabit this delightful place of the river will make you better. I just know it! We will bring gifts for them when we return on your birthday. Maybe they will favor us."

"So far, the gods have not heard any of my prayers. I'm wondering if they ever will," Meryt sighs.

"Your birthday is only five days from today. This will be a big day! You will want to feel refreshed for the grand party we are planning for you. We will be sure to come back here on the morning of your birthday. Won't that be fun?"

"I wish I could be excited. I have nothing to celebrate."

"You have much to celebrate, dear. The plans for your party are almost complete. Everyone is eagerly looking forward to your celebration. You must not disappoint your friends. When you have bathed at this beautiful place, you certainly will feel ready for the party. "

When the royal party has settled on board, the cedar boat heads up the river toward the city.

Chapter 13:
Deception and Discovery

"In the shadow of thy wings, I will take refuge, till the storms of destruction pass by, I cry to God Most High, to God who fulfills his purpose for me."

Psalms 57:1-2

Mahala feels the strain of sleepless nights. The baby has been restless for the past week. The tension of keeping him quiet is taking its toll on the family. Each adult takes a turn at night walking and patting him to settle him, hoping he will sleep. They rise in the morning feeling sluggish and exhausted.

Gritting her teeth against the pain in her pounding head, Mahala wonders aloud, "How will I get through this day?" She longs for a short time of uninterrupted quiet to take a nap in the refreshing, cool corner of the house. A nap is not possible with the three children in her care.

Carrying the baby in a sling wrapped closely at her breast, Mahala fights off the fatigue as she goes about her morning duties.

"Miriam, pat out these loaves for me. I am tending Baby Brother so he will not cry."

Miriam hurries to do as she is told. "I am a good helper. I can make good bread loaves. Can I hold my little brother when I am finished?" asks Miriam eager to please her grandmother.

"Yes. You are a good helper. We must not let your brother cry. When you are finished, you can hold him while I cook the bread. We must not let anyone know we have a baby here. Will you keep this secret?"

Mahala asks her granddaughter this question every day. She always receives an affirmative answer. She deliberately makes the question a habit. Repetition is the key. The children must not forget her instructions.

"I have not told even one person. I did not tell Grandmother Hogla or anyone. I will never, never tell. He is my secret brother."

"I am happy to know you will not tell anyone about our secret baby because this is very, very important. Do not forget what I tell you." Mahala admonishes.

"I help too. I take care secret brother, too," Aaron chimes in dancing around his grandmother.

Mahala manages a tired smile and reminds herself to be patient with Aaron's energy.

When Miriam has finished patting out the loaves, she sits on the ground with her legs crossed. Mahala places the baby in her lap. Little Brother enjoys his sister's attention. Miriam entertains the baby with songs and stories she spontaneously composes. He giggles and laughs when his sister tickles his chin.

Mahala goes back to her work.

Aaron picks up a stick and runs in circles around the fire pit, squealing and twirling the stick. The waving stick is creating a hazard as he gets closer and closer to the pit. His energy and noise are becoming annoying. Fatigue overcomes Mahala's patience.

"Aaron, put that stick down! Stop that squealing! People will hear you! Find something else to play. You will get us into trouble."

Aaron drops the stick and goes to the far corner of the courtyard where he wanders around looking for something to play.

Since Pharaoh's order to take all male infants, the children no longer play freely in the courtyards. They are confined to the farthest corner out of public view. Every day Aaron is cautioned to stay far away from the gate to avoid being seen by anyone who may be spying through the cracks and spaces between the post and the gate.

Without his sister's watchful eyes, he feels the freedom to roam. It is not long until he finds himself wandering toward the gate.

He looks back first toward Mahala then Miriam. Seeing they are still preoccupied with other matters, he moves further toward the tantalizing gate which continues to beckon him.

Looking back periodically to see who is watching, he slowly approaches. Peering through a crack between the wooden slats, he is startled to see a face looking back at him. He draws back frightened and starts to run away.

"Well, hello, Aaron. It's your Grandma Abahail and Aunt Orpha. We have come to see you. Will you let us in?"

Aaron peeps through the crack again. He stares at them for a minute and then shakes his head, saying, "No."

He turns to run away again when Abahail calls him back.

"Aaron! Come back. Look I brought some figs dried with honey just for you. They are very sweet. Would you like one?"

She opens the lid of a decorated basket to show the sweet figs inside. Holding the basket close to the crack, so he can smell the fragrant fruit, she makes a proposal.

"You can have one of these sweet, yummy figs if you will pull that basket to the gate, climb on it, and open the latch."

The boy looks at the sweet treats for a moment. The sweet smell tickles his nose. "Okay," he says as he turns and runs to get the basket.

Pulling the empty storage basket to the gate, he turns it upside down, climbs on it, and heaves up the latch.

Abahail pushes the gate open and comes in. "Good boy! You are a good helper. Is your mother home?" she asks as she offers him a fig.

"No. Her working." Aaron takes a fig from the basket and bites off a piece.

"Is she still sick?" Abahail asks innocently.

No, not sick. Went to work. You come to see secret brother?" Aaron talks with a mouth full of sticky fig.

"What did you say? Did you say something about a brother?" Abahail stoops closer to him. "Tell me again."

"Aaron!" Mahala, realizing Aaron has wandered toward the gate looks up to see Abahail standing inside the gate. Too late she sees that Aaron has opened the latch.

"Aaron, come here!" A sick feeling in the pit of her stomach overwhelms her. She puts her hands on either side of her head as she tries to control her emotions.

Followed by Orpha, Abahail quickly crosses the courtyard to where Mahala is working.

"Hello, Mahala, dear. Do we have a secret? Have you been keeping secrets from us? I suspected as much when you told us Jochebed was sick. I thought it was strange, especially when you wouldn't let us come and see her. She has always been such a strong girl."

Coming close to Mahala's personal space, Abahail points her finger toward Mahala's face "You should have told me. Did you think I would tell anybody? Didn't you trust me? We could have kept the secret together. Let me see my new grandson."

She stoops near Miriam and looks closely at the baby. "My, isn't he cute? When did he come? He looks to be over a month old."

"He is my secret brother. I take good care of him," Miriam say. "You are not supposed to tell anyone about him. Not even Grandfather Kohath."

"Oh, I promise. I will not tell a soul!" Abahail says raising her hands and then dramatically crossing her arms across her chest. "When did you say he came?"

Mahala's eyes dart from side to side. Her face is turned to the side away from Abahail. She feels like a trapped rabbit at the mercy of a hungry predator.

"He is three months old. We have not told anyone at all about him. Only those who live in this house know. It is too dangerous. Please understand why we have been so secretive. Please do not tell anyone. Please, please do not tell. Will you promise not to tell anyone?"

"Of course, we will not tell anybody, dear." Abahail's eyes gleam through narrow slits. A sardonic smile parts her lips slightly. Her face is like that of a wolf closing in on easy prey.

"Do you, for one minute, think I would betray my own husband's family? Don't you trust me? Do I know any Egyptian priests? Do I know any Egyptian soldiers? Will Orpha tell? Of course not! Orpha, we will not tell, will we?"

With a puckered face and lips making a downward motion at the corners, Orpha shakes her head, "No."

"Thank you, thank you, Abahail, I will always be grateful if you will not tell anyone. We really need your help during these hard times. I will do anything for you if you do not say anything about this baby to anyone. Just let me know what you need." Mahala grasps her thumb and presses her hands hard against her chest.

"Mahala, you act as if you do not believe us. Just to show how sincere I am, here, look I brought you some figs. They are large and very sweet. We dried them with honey. I even put them in a pretty basket for you." She puts the basket of figs on the ground near Miriam. "I will come back in a few days and bring a gift for my new grandson. We must be going. Say "Hello" to Jochebed and Amram. Bye for now. See you soon!"

Abahail can hardly restrain her feet from dancing as she goes toward the gate. She holds her breath to prevent herself from shouting for joy. With Orpha following behind her, she swings the gate open and with a flourish shuts it soundly behind Orpha.

"Orpha, the gods are finally favoring us! At last, we have a chance to get justice for all the wrongs our family has suffered! Your brothers will be very happy to know they may not have to serve Amram anymore!"

"Are you going to tell my brothers?" Orpha asks.

"Of course, I am! We have a perfect right to get justice for these wrongs!" Abahail says jubilantly.

"I don't think you should tell anyone about the baby. Remember you promised you would not tell. That would not be right," Orpha says in a quiet voice.

Abahail stops and turns toward her daughter. "What? Don't you know what those people have done to us? Hogla stole my husband. Amram stole the leadership position from your brothers, and Jochebed took Amram from you. We have every right to get even with them. Your brothers will see justice is done!" She clenches her teeth and folds her arms over her chest.

Orpha replies in a timid voice, "I know you have always wanted me to marry Amram, but I never wanted to marry him. He likes to be in front of people, and he has big ideas. The people expect the leader's wife to be beautiful. They talk about her and compare all other women to her. I don't want that."

Abahail is incredulous. "What are you saying? You are not angry about this injustice?"

"No, I do not want to marry Amram. I want to marry a man who is quiet like me. I want a man who will talk to me. Amram doesn't know I am alive. Since we were small children, everyone knew Amram intended to marry Jochebed. I never want to marry a man who is in love with another woman. I have already said that to you many times. And I don't want to think that I caused a baby to die!" Orpha raises her voice and looks directly at her mother.

"Where did you get these ideas, girl? This is nonsense! I am your mother! Don't I always know what is good for you? Men do not talk to their wives. They only visit them when they think the time is right for a pregnancy. The rest of their time is spent talking business with other men. We women must help ourselves. It is a woman's responsibility to advance herself and her children. Now come on. We have work to do." Abahail turns her back and walks faster toward home.

Later in the afternoon when Jochebed and Sarah return from the fields, Mahala relates the dreaded discovery with tears in her eyes.

"I am so sorry! I feel so very bad. I was not watching Aaron very well. It is my fault. If they come to take Little Brother, I will be to blame. I will never forgive myself."

She weeps. "Oh! How I hope we can trust her not to tell. I I am so sorry! I will never forgive myself!"

Jochebed tries to comfort her mother-in-law. "I know she will tell her sons who will report to the Egyptians. But don't blame yourself. Abahail has been trying to find out what we are doing for many months. She has been snooping around the village asking everyone about us. She must have been watching every day to see into this courtyard by looking through the crack in the gate. It was just a matter of time before she discovered our secret."

Terror starts to rise in the girl's voice as she says, "That awful woman took advantage of a three-year-old boy to get into our house. It is not your fault. She would sooner or later find out. She will tell her sons. They will tell the Egyptians just to get even with Amram."

When Amram hears the story, he hugs his mother and comforts her with a few words saying it was not her fault. Then abruptly he takes his weapons and leaves the house.

Jochebed feels the panic welling up in her stomach. It was the same panic that gripped her when she heard the horses and chariots on that Terrible Day. Prickles run up her spine as the hair stands up on the back of her head.

"This means we have only a few days to think of a plan to save Little Brother. What can we do?" she says to herself as she clasps the infant to her breast and begins to pace around and around the courtyard. With every step, her confusion, rage, and fear grow. Memories of the Terrible Day return with fury to haunt her to near hysteria.

When the night is falling, she withdraws to the roof to nurse the baby. As the calming sensation of nursing takes effect, her mind leaves those horrible recollections and returns to the present. All is peaceful outwardly. The infant is innocently suckling at her breast and making quiet little noises as he takes his nourishment. Her eyes look up to the stars as each makes its appearance one after the other. The familiar little lights seem to greet her with sparkling cheerfulness as multitudes of winking stars fill the sky.

Mahala brings Aaron and Miriam to their beds. When they are asleep, she returns to the room below to join Sarah. They are too distraught to try to sleep.

Jochebed sits with the baby and watches the stars.

"Are you watching me now?" she softly prays. "Thank you for saving Aaron. I was so afraid he would die. Thank you for sending Little Brother. He is such a special child. Now I must hide him. Is it possible to hide a small baby? Where are the hiding places that can keep him safe for a few years? Will you help me save him? I am so helpless. Please, please, help me. I just can't let him die. I will do anything. Do you really care what is happening? How can I know you are here when I can't see or hear you? How can I be certain you are here?"

She searches the length and breadth of the unending universe for answers. No answers are seen in the deep and starry sky. The sound of the sleeping child's quiet breathing, his pixie face so serene and beautiful in the light of a rising moon, reminds her how precious and fragile this little life really is.

"He is a special child. At birth, he was blessed. This must mean he is more important than even my own wishes to hold on to him," she muses. "Great God, since you gave me this special child, you will surely help me save him. What must I do? What must I do?"

Her thoughts flit here and there searching, asking, and seeking for answers. She reviews the day's events remembering how the mother bird so efficiently hides her nest right under the eyes of the hawk. Is there a simple solution to hiding a child as efficiently as a common bird hides her nest?

Images of the boat coming onto shore with the royal party rise in her head. As she remembers the princess who is depressed over the loss of her child, the raging anger returns.

"So, this woman is depressed about the loss of one child. What about all our women who will never stop mourning the loss of many children? This is God's justice. The princess deserves to lose her child. Her father Pharaoh deserves to lose all his grandchildren. All the Egyptians should have to endure what they caused us to suffer. I hope all of them go through all the pain they put on us." she whispers aloud.

The moon illuminates the angelic, tiny face with its gentle silver glow. She lightly brushes his soft hair and feels his plump little arms. With her finger, she traces his facial features and studies each perfect little detail of the sleeping child.

"You are too beautiful to die now. You are so special. I want to keep you forever. I want to see you grow to be a handsome man. You will not grow to be a man unless I find a way to hide you right under old Pharaoh's eyes. You will be lost like so many others if I try to keep you here."

She thinks for a long time. Then a plan takes shape. It is a bold plan, so risky and daring it is frightening to think about it. At first, she dismisses it as foolish, much too dangerous and uncertain. After weighing all the risks over and over, she knows what she must do.

"In order to save you, I will have to give you up because in this village death is certain. There is only one place where you can hide right under Pharaoh's eyes."

She strokes his little face with her finger.

"It is a very big gamble, but it may be the only way. The time is short. I must plan carefully."

Her body shakes as if from cold. Her hands tremble as she scans the sky.

"I am terrified. Is this what you want me to do, Great God?" she asks as she scans the deep, immeasurable universe, Is this your plan for him? I trust this is your plan. Even if I become a sacrificial lamb, I must trust this is your will."

Sarah, Mahala, and the children are still asleep when the sun peeps over the distant mountains. Jochebed stirs from her restless, brief sleep and wakes the baby for his early morning feeding. When he has finished, she wraps him in his softest blanket and descends the stairs.

In the courtyard she sees Amram sitting on a wooden bench with his broad back toward her. His head bowed, his face in his hands, he is the picture of despondency. She has never seen him like this before. The sight makes a lump come into her throat.

Slowly and quietly, she approaches her husband and sits beside him.

"Have you been here very long?"

"For a while. It was no use trying to sleep."

"I know. Did you find any of your friends to guard this house?"

Turning his gaze toward her he says, "No. If it were only my uncles, I would be able to deal with this, but I cannot fight Pharaoh's army. I know my uncles will inform the Egyptians as soon as they can contact the right officials. They want to let Pharaoh's army do their dirty work."

A look of desperation comes across his face.

"I can't ask my men to risk their lives to save my son when they have lost their own sons. Besides, if we fight, they will kill all of us. They will take all our children and our wives as well. Pharaoh will call any violence an insurrection and send the entire army to this village to make an example of us. He is afraid of a rebellion. He will use a fight as an excuse to kill many innocent people. My uncles know this. They want to get rid of not only me but also my men and their families as well. It will be all of us!"

He turns away and covers his face with his hands to hide his emotions.

He speaks through his fingers, "Jochie, I have never felt so helpless in my life. I do not know what to do. I have spent all night thinking and I have no answers. Everything I think of turns to a dead end."

When he looks up his face shows deep lines of exhaustion. He runs his fingers through his thick dark hair, making it stand out from his head.

Though he does not expect an answer, he asks with a hopeless sigh, "Do you have any ideas about what we can do?"

She waits long minutes before speaking.

"Last night a plan came to me. I believe this plan could have come from the Almighty. I do not know for sure. It may be foolish, but it is the only plan I can think about."

Taking her hand in his, he says gently, "So tell me, what plan did the Almighty send to you?"

She explains in detail the plan that formed in her mind during the night and waits for his response.

His eyes become wide; his jaw drops open.

"That's crazy! Only a woman could think of that! It almost makes me want to laugh."

His facial expressions move from amusement, doubt, fear, and finally admiration.

"Huh. It's so crazy it may work. It could buy some time, but it is a very big risk."

He ponders for a moment.

"This plan could be very dangerous not only for the baby but for all of us. I will mull it over for a few hours and let you know if we will proceed with it, but this may be the only plan we have."

Chapter 14:
The Daring Scheme

"Let this be recorded for a generation to come, so that a people yet unborn may praise the Lord: that he looked down from his holy height, from heaven the Lord looked at the earth, to hear the groans of the prisoners, to set free those who were doomed to die: that men may declare in Zion the name of the Lord."

Psalms 102:18-21

"This will be the most important basket I ever weave. It must be perfect. I cannot afford any mistakes. This has got to work," Jochebed says to Sarah and Mahala as her hands move swiftly to weave a basket in the shape of a boat.

"Amram agreed to this since he says he knows there is no other way. He was not happy at first. He said it is very risky. But as he thought about it, he agreed to get pitch and tar to make this basket as watertight as Noah's ark. It will have a lid with openings in it to let in the light."

At times she stops weaving to measure the size and get it just right to carry its precious cargo. Mahala, Sarah, and Miriam carefully select dry reeds and place them within easy reach to save time in weaving. The family works with frantic urgency.

When the weaving is complete, Jochebed daubs the sticky black tar onto the reeds to seal any cracks. She coats the inside and outside, allows it to dry, and repeats the process two more times. By the third day, it is completed.

Very early in the morning on the fifth day, Jochebed and Miriam are headed up the river with Miriam carrying the special basket. Jochebed is carrying Little Brother wrapped in a linen coverlet and a lambskin.

"This is a very, very important mission, Miriam. Listen carefully. You must be sure to say just what I tell you. Will you do this for Little Brother?"

"Oh, yes, I can do it. I know I can do it." Miriam dances with excitement enjoying the drama of such an adventure.

Carefully, Jochebed describes her plan of action in meticulous detail. She tells about the bright-colored boat with its curved bow and fringed canopy and the Egyptian men who are rowing it. Next Jochebed paints a word picture of the princess.

"Our plan will work best if you talk to the princess. She wears a lot of golden jewelry and a very pretty dress. She seems nice, and you must be very nice when you talk to her. Bow to her like this."

Jochebed bows to show how it is done. "We do not want her to get angry with you. You must smile and be very kind. You must watch and listen very carefully so you will know when to talk."

"The queen will be there to help the princess. The queen wears a beautiful robe and has a big, black wig with straight hair. Serving maids who help the princess will be there as well." Jochebed makes a gesture with her hands to describe the large wig.

"When they find the basket and open it, wait to see what the princess says about the baby. If she seems happy, listen carefully to what they say. Listen to see if she wants someone to nurse the baby. You must not come out too early or things may not go well. You must wait until you know you can talk to the princess before you come out from your hiding place."

The young mother stoops to look her daughter in the face. "Now tell me what you must do when it is time for you to ask if the princess will need a person to nurse the baby."

Miriam repeats everything her mother has said.

"That is very good. Do not forget what we talked about." Looking her daughter steadily in the eyes, she says, "Remember we may have to wait for a long time before the boat comes, so do not get impatient. Just wait quietly. This is very important."

When they reach the bathing place at the river's edge, Miriam is instructed to hide in the reeds close to the shore near a log, close to the stone bench. She waits patiently for the drama to begin.

Leaving Mirium in her hiding place, Jochebed carefully studies the tall papyrus growing beyond the bathing area a short distance from the shore. She gently places the baby in his specially designed waterproof container. Pulling the floating basket behind her, the young mother wades into the river until the water reaches her chest.

"See, this is your little boat. You are taking a ride. Isn't this fun?" she croons to the baby. When she reaches a place where the basket can be partially hidden, but still visible from the shore, she steadies the basket against the reeds "Do not be afraid. When you come out, you will be a prince. Do not cry, little one. You will be a mighty prince," she says softly, holding his tiny hands. "Be brave. You must be brave".

After a last kiss, his beautiful face disappears as she closes the lid. She stares at her little creation of straw covered in pitch for a moment, longing to take the infant from his little ark and go home.

When he starts to whimper, her heart sinks, yet she has no choice but to turn toward the shore and leave the child to his fate.

"Crocodiles may be lurking nearby! I may never see him again!" She whispers as tears start to flow. "Oh, Almighty God! You are my last hope! Can you see me? Will you keep your promise to our ancient father? I beg you to save my baby! I can't bear to lose him!"

When she steps onto the beach, the only thing left for her to do is wait in agony to see what will happen to her baby and her dream.

After a long while, the slender, cedar boat appears. It comes directly onto the beach. Nephre seems more tired, as if she has not slept. The entire party appears to be in a somber mood.

The princess remains in the boat until the others have moved onto the beach. Fazel holds out his hand to help her, but she sits still. She appears even more subdued than before.

"Come, Meryt, dear, the cool water will cheer you up. Don't you want to bathe?" Nephre entreats her, "Please do this for me. It will help you. Remember you want to be ready for the party tonight."

Slowly the dejected girl gets out. "I'm not looking forward to this party. Everyone knows I have failed. They will try to say nice things to me, but I know they are laughing at me behind my back. Do I have to go? Why did they plan this? They should know I don't want it. They just wanted an excuse to throw a party for their own fun."

"That's not true, dear. Your friends want to honor you on your birthday. They love you as you are. You have not failed. You are still young; you may yet have a child. Let's ask the gods again to give you a child. We brought more offerings this time."

After the offerings and the preparations for bathing are completed, Meryt enters the river and starts to dabble in the water. She wanders aimlessly toward the reeds where the basket waits and then stops suddenly. "What is that I hear? It sounds like some poor animal or a baby crying. It is coming from over there. Look! There is something near those reeds. What is it?"

"It looks like a small ark. What can it be? Who would leave something like that here?" Nephre wonders.

"Titi, go get it. I want to see what it is," the princess commands.

"No, dear, that might be dangerous. Leave it alone," the Queen cautions.

"I want to see what is in that little ark! Titi, Get it for me!" Meryt commands more firmly.

The queen gives up with a shrug of her shoulders. Titi wades to the basket and pulls it to the princess. Loud cries are coming from within the basket. Titi carefully opens the lid. Little Brother frightened and alone, is crying vigorously waving his little fists. His face is red from crying for so long. The women stare at the distraught child completely shocked to see an infant left to float in the river.

"Look! It's a baby! Who would leave a baby here? Why would anyone leave their baby here in a basket in this river? This is very strange!" Titi exclaims.

"There must be something wrong with it. No one would leave their child alone in a basket. There are crocodiles in this river," Nuti says.

"Nuti, take the baby out so I can see it," the princess speaks firmly.

Nuti lifts the infant from the basket, sponges him off, and wraps him in a linen cloth. She holds the crying baby up for Meryt to see.

"This is one of the Hebrews' children," Nuti says.

"Bring him over here. I want to hold him," Meryt commands. She goes to the bench and sits down. Titi smooths a blanket across Meryt's knees then places the baby on her lap. Delighted, the princess wipes the tears from his face.

"Who left you here, baby? Oh, you are a poor, poor little baby, don't cry. There, there, I will take care of you. You are safe now. You are going to be all right now that I have found you." The princess croons as she gently bounces him on her knees until he stops crying and looks at her with his beautiful eyes.

"Oh look. He is so beautiful. Look! How cute you are, baby!" The princess laughs aloud. The women gather close to get a good look at the foundling child. One by one they comment on what a beautiful child he is.

"My Lady, this is a Hebrew baby," Fazel nods toward Meryt. "Your father will not…"

"Of course, you can keep him. They left him here. That means they do not want him. He can be yours," Nephre says flatly, cutting Fazel short with a withering look.

Titi and Nuti's eyes meet. They give each other a nod.

"What a fine baby he is. We will help you care for him. We will see that he has everything he needs. He looks hungry. Who will nurse him?" Titi asks. The women look from one to the other and shrug.

Suddenly Miriam is standing at the princess's elbow. Until this moment, everyone in the royal party was too distracted by the baby to notice Miriam as she quietly slipped from her hiding place and approached the group.

Alarmed and frustrated by his oversight, Fazel jumps toward the girl to grab her away from the princess. Nephre raises her hand as a signal for Fazel to stop. She waves and nods to Miriam, giving her permission to approach the princess.

"Would you like for me to find a Hebrew nurse for the baby?" Miriam asks, as she bows politely.

"Oh, I did not see you, little girl. Do you know a Hebrew nurse?" Meryt asks with eager excitement.

"Yes, Your Majesty. I do know a nurse. May I bring one for you?" Miriam bows once more.

"What a sweet little girl you are. That would be wonderful! Please go quickly. You came at just the right time."

The princess is all smiles.

"Just when I need a nurse, she offers to bring one. How fortunate! Mother, this is my lucky day. The gods have already answered our prayer!" Meryt says happily.

"Yes, Meryt, dear, the gods are hearing your prayers," Nephre responds with a sparkling smile as she claps her hands together.

Miriam bows once more, "I will return very soon with a nurse, Your Majesty." She turns and runs toward the village.

Fazel leads Nephre aside out of ear shot from the others.

"My Queen, please listen to me. Please consider the fact that allowing Lady Meryt to keep this baby is not a good idea. The Pharaoh will not be happy about this Hebrew baby. You know those shepherd people are not allowed to live in the royal courts. There is no reason to cause the princess any more pain by telling her she can keep this baby. Keeping the baby will bring more sorrow and grief for her. We should leave it here. Someone will come for it."

Nephre straightens her back. She raises her chin. Her words are determined and firmly stated.

"Now that we know about this baby, soldiers will come for him and kill him. I know all about the king's command to slay Hebrew children. Did he think he would keep so big a secret from me? My daughter knows about the command to kill babies, too. She has a very tender heart. She will never recover if she thinks this baby will be killed. We cannot leave him here."

Fazel makes another attempt to reason with the Queen.

"That little girl did not come here by accident. She is going to bring the baby's mother and possibly a band of Hebrew outlaws as well. We may be in great danger. The Pharaoh has trusted me, his faithful servant, with your safety."

Fazel raises his hands clasped in a praying motion. "You, his queen, and his precious daughter, mean the whole world to him. I must not fail him. I beg you, please, please, persuade Lady Meryt to put the baby back in the basket and return it to the river. She cannot take a chance to make her father angry. She is putting herself in great danger by thinking she will keep this baby."

"She will have more grief knowing if she returns the baby to the river he will be killed. She will never live over losing two babies. Fazel, look at her."

Nephre waves toward the princess who is singing softly to the wide-eyed infant.

"I have not seen her smile like this in two years. Her pain is gone. The light is back in her eyes. She has come out of her darkness. If this child can make her so happy, he is truly a gift from the gods. He was sent in answer to our prayers. Is this not so?"

The queen raises her hands and places them on either side of her face, Her eyes are determined, her voice soft but firm.

"The mother must be desperate to save the child. If she is willing to give up her son to save him, she must be a noble woman. I will always be in debt to her. As for Pharaoh, you and I will convince him to give his consent to keep this tiny baby who has already done more for our daughter than all our wise men. He is the only one who has been able to bring Meryt out of her sorrow. We must not allow her to lose this baby too. Keeping this child may be her only hope. We must do all we know to help her keep him. Her life may depend on it. I am willing to take any risk whether it is with outlaws or the king's anger. For my daughter it is a small thing I can do."

"As you wish, My Queen. I am not convinced this is a good idea. It has its risks for both of us." Fazel answers pulling the corners of his mouth downward and shaking his head no.

Miriam returns, followed by her mother.

"I found a nurse, Your Majesty." The little girl announces as she dances toward Meryt.

Jochebed approaches the princess slowly, keeping her eyes on the ground.

"Oh, you are back so quickly, little girl," Meryt says, barely glancing toward Jochebed as she coos to the baby.

Jochebed hesitantly addresses the princess without raising her eyes. "Your Majesty, this little girl says you called for my services?"

"Yes. Yes, I did. Do you nurse infants?" the princess asks, eagerly.

"Yes, Your Majesty. I have plenty of milk for a healthy infant."

The young mother keeps her eyes on the ground, away from the baby. She does not want to show any sign she recognizes him. She prays he will not start to cry when he hears her voice.

"I will pay you well to nurse him until he is old enough to wean."

"As you wish, Your Majesty. I will nurse him for you."

"Take him now; he seems to be hungry. I will send a messenger to you to let you know when I want to see how he is getting along. You will bring him here, so I can visit him at this place until he is weaned." The princess kisses the baby on his head and his cheeks and then hands him to Jochebed.

"Goodbye, sweet baby. I will come check on you again." Pharaoh's daughter takes a gold bracelet from her wrist and holds it out to Jochebed.

"Take this bracelet. It has a royal inscription on it. It will be a symbol of my protection. I will not let anyone harm you or the baby. If anyone threatens you show the inscription on this bracelet."

Jochebed takes the bracelet and slips it on her arm. "Thank you, Your Majesty. You are very kind. I will take very good care of this baby for you."

She bows and turns toward the village with Miriam following.

The royal party boards the boat. As the craft pulls away from the shore, Meryt gazes back toward the shore, her face joyful with a radiant smile.

"My prayers have been answered! Thank you! Thank you to all the great gods of the river. What a wonderful gift you have given to me. I am so happy! I thought I could never be happy again! I asked for a son; now I will have one! Tonight, I will dance for joy!"

She raises her hands in a triumphant gesture. "What a wonderful birthday gift! At last, I will celebrate my birthday with dancing and music! Listen, you sisters who mock me behind my back! You will not make fun of me anymore! I will be a mother. You and your sons will bow to my son! You wait and see!"

Chapter 15:
Doubt, Fear and Anger

"In God, I have put my trust; I will not fear. What can flesh do to me?"

Psalms 56:4

The baby sleeps restlessly on the lambskin. Mahala, carrying a jar of water, comes into the room. She finds her daughter-in-law weeping as if her heart will break. "What is wrong, Child? You act as if all is lost," Mahala asks with a mother's concern. "I thought you would be happy since Little Brother is safe for now.

"Oh-oh," Jochebed sniffs through sobs.

"I feel so bad! My milk is drying up. Little Brother did not get enough milk. He cried himself to sleep. He will wake up hungry very soon. What will I do? How will I be able to nurse him? Even though he is safe for the present, he may die if I have no milk."

"Why is your milk drying up? You had no trouble nursing Miriam and Aaron?" Mahala patiently places the water jar in the cool corner of the room.

"My milk is going away because I am so angry. My body doesn't want to eat or drink. This anger keeps telling me I will have to give up my son. I hate the princess who is going to take my baby!

She raises her arm to grasp her hair. Light from the window strikes the wide golden band on her arm. A brilliant flash of light from the gold bracelet briefly illuminates the room.

"I hate wearing this stupid bracelet! It keeps reminding me of that skinny Egyptian woman. I do not want anyone to know I have it." She covers it with her sleeve.

She continues to wail. "I haven't told anyone about it. I don't want anyone to know about it. Some want to believe we are making deals with the Egyptians. They may say we took gold for information about other people's children. I hate Pharaoh because he is so wicked! He killed so many innocent children. He killed my best friend and her family."

Her voice becomes louder as her face twists with anger. "And I hate Abahail because she tricked Aaron into letting her in our courtyard. I could have kept my baby hidden longer. But she just wanted to hurt us. We did not do anything to her. Orpha went along with her. That girl does everything her mother tells her to do. She is guilty as well. I hate her too! I wish they were dead."

Mahala interrupts her. There, there, child. You must calm down. You cannot allow your milk to fail. You cannot allow Little Brother to go hungry."

Mahala tries to calm the distraught young woman. She sits down on a lambskin next to her and prepares to listen to her complaints.

Jochebed continues her rant. "I am not a good mother! I am not a good person! I lied to everyone about my bracelet. Teenagers did not threaten me. Young men did not take the bracelet. Everyone believed me and felt sorry for me, but I was lying! I was stupid! I gave the bracelet to a soothsayer hoping she would tell me how to save Aaron, but she just tricked me. I foolishly lost that beautiful family treasure. When I think of how easily she deceived me, I am so ashamed. I feel such loss!" Sobbing, she wipes tears from her face with her hands, but more tears flow.

She sniffs as her speech overflows with self-pity. "Miriam will not have a marriage bracelet when she is betrothed. I am a stupid liar! How can I ever bring up these children when I am so stupid? How can I tell Miriam and Aaron to be truthful when I am a liar? Trying to be a good mother is just too hard when all these bad things are happening."

Mahala interrupts the speech. "Dry your tears, child. Dry your tears. You cannot afford to carry these burdens you are placing on yourself. You have been pouting for four days. Your milk is drying because of it. Anger, jealousy, fear, guilt, and hatred are very heavy loads. You cannot do your work when you are weighed down with these burdens. Put these things aside. You cannot afford to drag these things around with you."

Jochebed stops sobbing and looks at her mother-in-law. Mahala's face is firm. Her mouth is set. She looks steadily at her daughter-in-law.

Resuming her tirade, Jochebed says, " I am just so furious. It is too hard to stop being angry. I must give up my precious son. That painted-faced, awful woman will turn my beautiful son into a cruel and evil Egyptian. When I think about how unfair this is, I want to kill her. I am so angry and afraid. It is just not fair! I will never get over it."

Again, Mahala patiently attempts to calm her. "I know; I know terrible things have happened. Certainly, you do have reason to be angry. But what will your anger do for you? Will your anger change anything that happened or make all the bad things go away?"

"No, I suppose it will not make anything that has happened go away," Jochebed says slowly.

Mahala immediately responds, "Then tell me what will it do for you?"

"I don't know!" the young woman says. " I keep thinking about all these things. The more I think, the angrier I get. Why shouldn't I be angry? It is just not fair! I will be angry for the rest of my life. I can't stand it. I will never forgive any of them. Do you think anything that has happened to me is fair?"

"I did not say life is fair," Mahala raises her voice slightly. "I know very well that life is not fair. I did not live this long and fail to see that terrible things happen when it is not our fault. And I know very well that there are people who should help us, but they want to hurt us instead. This hurt is very hard, but we must learn to deal with it. We must not let them turn us into angry, bitter people."

Mahala's voice becomes firmer. "I want to know if I will have to spend the rest of my life in this house with an angry bitter woman. That certainly won't be pleasant!"

She continues with a firmer voice. "You hate Abahail. But do you want to be like her? She carries her anger with her always. Do you want your children to be like hers? Her children are miserable because they are filled with anger and jealousy. Do you plan to fill our house with this? Will you make all of us miserable?"

Mahala is usually patiently sympathetic to the young woman's complaints, but these words are stinging.

"Are you saying I have no right to be angry?" Jochebed asks weakly.

"No. I did not say that. It is not right that you must give up your baby. But you must know your angry feelings and your guilty feelings are your worst enemies. You cannot hold onto them. These feelings will destroy us all. Your mission is too important. Life is very hard, but this is not a reason to make it harder. Your children's lives are in your hands. You must do your best for them."

"Do you expect me to feel good about having to give up my baby? Do you think I can be happy when so many bad things have happened to me?" Jochebed raises her voice.

"No," Mahala answers softly, "I do not expect you to be happy about losing your son or any of the other bad things that have happened to you and the other mothers, but how will your anger change any of these things?"

Placing her hands on her hips, Mahala looks down at her daughter-in-law. "The princess feels nothing because you are angry with her. She makes people angry every day and feels nothing. She does not care that you are angry. The Pharaoh does not care whether any of our people live or die. Your anger certainly will not hurt him."

Mahala pauses and breathes a sigh. "Your anger will only hurt you and our family. It will poison all of us. Is holding onto your anger worth that?"

Folding her arms across her chest, she continues, "Abahail will clap for joy if she sees how angry you are. Do you want to see her gleeful face laughing at your anger every time you are around her? Do you want to hear her cackling laughter because she knows she successfully hurt you and Amram? You must not be like her."

Mahala turns toward the door. "You must not let your anger destroy your life and your children's lives. Do not let these burdens of anger, guilt, and bitterness keep you from doing your best work. Dry your tears. That is enough crying."

Pausing, then turning toward her task, Mahala says slowly, "It is time to remember you have a mission. You have been through much sorrow, pain, and hardship, but you are not stupid, a liar, or an incompetent person. When a person is desperate and afraid, bad people come to take advantage of him or her because these bad people know the desperate person has clouded judgment."

Large earthen pots each containing either wheat, barley, or millet rest in the corner. With a small bowl, Mahala scoops up the required amount of grain for grinding a supply of flour for the day's supply of bread. Pouring it into her clay bowl, she stands, bowl on her hip, continuing her conversation.

"The desperate person can be led to do things he or she would never do if his or her thoughts were clear. You were deceived but you are not a foolish woman. You are a strong woman, and you will be stronger. With God's help, you will succeed."

Mahala picks up her jar of oil and goes to the courtyard to start preparations for the next meal.

The young mother sits for a while mulling over what she has heard. She starts to pray to the Almighty.

"It is hard to admit, but Mahala is right. There is nothing I can do if others plot evil. I must do everything possible to see my baby survive. Anger, fear, sorrow, or hardship must not be allowed to burden the family or deter me from my mission. Please renew my strength to go forward. Please help me to keep my mission."

Her experience with nursing her first two children taught her to eat and drink more than usual if the milk started to dry up. Dipping into the water jar with a ladle made from a gourd, she drinks as much as she can hold and then searches for a piece of left-over bread and starts to eat.

Satisfied her body has the nourishment to produce enough milk, Jochebed picks up her son and attempts another feeding.

Suddenly the noise of horses' feet echoes through the village. A chariot carrying two men has stopped at the front gate.

The Egyptian commander shouts, "Open this gate!"

Mahala runs to obey the command.

A burly Egyptian soldier wearing a helmet jumps out of the chariot and brushes past Mahala as he strides toward the house. Jochebed screams in terror when he bursts through the door. He seizes the baby from her arms and pushes her violently to the floor as she tries to stand. Grasping the shrieking child by his foot, he turns to leave.

Jochebed jumps to her feet and springs after him. With his free arm, he slaps her down again and resumes his stride toward the chariot where the commander waits.

The frantic mother scrambles to her feet and runs screaming hysterically. She catches up to him, but he pushes her to the ground for the third time and then steps up into the chariot.

With speed driven by desperation, Jochebed regains her feet, lunges toward the horse, and grabs the bridles on both sides of the animal's head. At the same time, the commander slaps the reins on the horse's rump commanding it to move forward. Confused, the animal rears and throws his head up raising the woman off the ground. Jochebed swings her body to the right narrowly avoiding the thrashing hooves.

The sleeve of her tunic falls to her shoulder exposing her arm as she clutches tighter on the horse's bridle. A brilliant flash of light blazes from her arm as sunlight strikes the golden bracelet.

Pharaoh's insignia inscribed on the gold band catches the commander's eye, sending shock waves up his spine and into his scalp. He freezes, transfixed, staring at the emblem as if it were a cobra rising a few feet in front of him poised and ready to strike.

The horse returns to its standing position and Jochebed finds her footing.

Hurdling himself over the side of the chariot, the commander grabs Jochebed's arm. He closely examines the bracelet. His eyebrows knot over his nose bridge and his face takes on a somber look. He drops Jochebed's arm.

Bellowing loud enough to be heard over the shrill screeches of the writhing child, he shouts, "Return the baby to her!"

Jochebed snatches her distressed son. Pressing his head to her breast, she runs toward the house ignoring the pain in her hip as she limps on her injured foot.

The commander assumes control of the chariot. He slaps the horse and orders, "Let's go!"

The men, horse, and chariot leave as suddenly as they appear.

Chapter 16:
Reconciliation and Hope

"He who covers his sins will not prosper, but whoever confesses and forsakes them will have mercy."

Proverbs 28:13

Only a few people saw the Egyptian soldiers and their chariot on the day screams of a terrified woman and a newborn baby were heard in the village. Rumors, most exaggerated, are whispered around the village. Speculation is growing that Jochebed was hiding a baby and the Egyptians captured her and her baby and took them away.

Amram refuses to discuss the matter, saying he cannot say anything about the alleged event at this time. The only information he will give is that Jochebed is at home recovering from a lingering illness. He stated he would call a council meeting with the family leaders when more information is available.

No one is sure what happened, but everyone is very uneasy as suspicions mount. Communication is in whispers to trusted family members and friends. An eerie unpleasant atmosphere saturates the air like a choking dust storm blowing across the desert.

Jochebed has not ventured outside the house since the chariot appeared two weeks ago. She remains secluded. Settling on a lambskin propped on her pillow, she sits in her designated corner preparing to give the baby his mid-morning feeding.

The baby eagerly takes his mother's breast and nurses contentedly as he makes soft grunting sounds. He falls asleep still nursing.

The young mother is startled when she looks up and sees a woman's form silhouetted in the doorway. The bright light from the outside contrasts with the darker interior of the room making it difficult to determine who the woman may be. She squints trying to recognize the identity of the silhouetted figure.

"Who is it?" Jochebed asks with alarm in her voice.

"Uhm…It is Orpha. May I uh…come in? Ah…Uh," a stuttering voice responds.

"Orpha?! What are you doing here? Who let you in?" Jochebed's alarm grows.

Orpha steps just inside the door.

"Mahala said I could come in. Ah. I know I have never come to see you before but… Ah… Um… I saw Mahala outside and let her know I had important things to say to you. Mahala said I could come to speak with you."

More alarmed, Jochebed says, "I have not seen anyone from the outside in more than two weeks. How did you get Mahala to agree that you could come in?" Questions whirl in Jochebed's mind. Has Mahala made another serious mistake by allowing the enemy into the house for the second time? What could be so important that Mahala could not simply take a message from Orpha?

"Uh. Ah. I let her know it is very important that I speak to you. I came because I promised Father that I would come and see you with my own eyes."

Orpha's eyes dart around the room. Her speech comes out in stammers and sputters. The nervous twisting of her head lets her head cover fall around her neck showing her straight brown hair that lays flat on her scalp and falls in unruly strands onto her shoulders.

"Uh. Mmm. Ah… Someone reported to him that the Egyptians took you away. Father became very depressed. He said he must know the truth before he can go on living. He made me swear I would tell him the truth. I let him know I would talk to you if you were still here. You see, Father's life depends on my speaking to you face to face. I had to know for sure that you are um.. well..still alive. I had to see you with my own eyes because he wanted to know for sure if you were, ah, um..if you had been captured. I must tell him the truth."

"Is my father well?" Questions continue to gnaw at the edges of Jochebed's brain. She studies Orpha's face hoping to unearth a clue if this visit is truly about Kohath's health or was it some other reason that prompted Orpha's sudden appearance?

"He will be better when he knows you are still alive and... ah.. at home," Orpha says keeping her eyes on the floor.

"Where is your mother?" Jochebed asks since Orpha rarely goes anywhere without her mother.

Orpha shuffles her feet while placing one hand over the other several times. She fidgets nervously. "She is not at home now. Did the Egyptians hurt you when they came to take your baby?"

"How do you know the Egyptians came to take my baby?" Jochebed asks suspiciously.

Orpha briefly glances at Jochebed before lowering her eyes. "Uh. Well. That is what I heard from really good sources. I do not know that for sure. That is one reason I came. Father wants to know what happened since there are many rumors, and you haven't been seen for a while."

"You may tell my father Amram and I will visit him when we are sure it is safe. Is my father able to walk and talk well?"

"Ah. Yes, but he needs to know you are okay before he will eat and talk again. I think he will recover when he knows for sure you were not captured, and I spoke to you personally. I am very glad they did not take your baby."

"Thank you," Jochebed says doubtfully.

"Uh. There are some things I need to say to you. May I sit down?" Orpha looks at Jochebed expectantly.

"What things?" Jochebed hesitates and then motions toward a woven rug and a cushion on the floor.

Orpha takes off her head covering and sits on the rug.

"Ok. Well. Uh. Yes. I just want you to know I never wanted to marry Amram."

Jochebed stares at Orpha. Not sure what she should say, she says nothing.

"Ah. Uh…I know my mother asked Father many times to give me as a bride to Amram, but I never wanted to marry him. I was very glad Father did not listen to her."

Orpha keeps her eyes on the floor. "I always thought about our ancient mother, Leah, the not-so-pretty sister, who married Jacob by deceiving him. I don't know if it was her fault, but she knew Jacob was in love with her sister, Rachael, but she married him despite it."

Orpha glances up and then down again. "Maybe Leah…um. thought she could make Jacob love her, but she couldn't. He did not love her. He did not respect her or her children. Her children did not respect him because he made no secret that he preferred Rachel's sons. I never want to marry a man when I know he is in love with another woman. I just want you to know that."

Jochebed studies her face and her awkward mannerisms. Orpha appears as one who is grappling with a heavy burden clinging to her shoulders. She is struggling to disentangle from it. Jochebed wonders what her half-sister is trying to tell her.

The baby wakes. He opens his eyes wide and coos to draw his mother's attention to himself. Jochebed looks into his eyes and strokes his cheek. His face breaks into a wide grin of innocent joy. He cackles a baby laugh as he kicks his feet and waves his tiny fists.

From the corner of her eye, Jochebed catches the look on Orpha's face in an unguarded moment. The look is one of intense longing. A maternal sound escapes from her throat. The sound is deep from within like an unexpected laugh between joy and distress. Her eyes are filled with pain; her mouth is drawn back and down as if a scab is suddenly being ripped from an unhealed wound.

Jochebed attempts to ease the awkward moment. "He often does this when he has finished his feeding. He lets me know he is happy."

Orpha's squirms. Her hands fly up to cover her eyes. With two or three deep breaths, she stifles her emotions. Over the years she has become skilled at covering her feelings. She recovers her composure. But her words come slowly with effort.

"I want so much to have a baby! Two years before your wedding Sahul asked Father to give him my hand in marriage. I was so excited that I may have the opportunity to have my own family. Father said Sahul is an honorable man. He was ready to give his consent, but Mother would not permit it. She said Sahul's family did not have the status I needed in a husband. I cried for weeks. It did no good. Mother never listens to me. I begged and pleaded with Mother for months, but it did no good. She never listens to me."

"That is too bad. You should be allowed to have a family like other women," Jochebed answers.

"Sahul waited two more years. He came back to ask again several times to see if Mother would change her mind. She did not. I still cry sometimes. When I go to the river to draw water, I see Sahul's wife and her children. It is hard for me to see her so content with her beautiful children. I know it is not her fault that I do not have children. I could not expect Sahul to remain unmarried because I couldn't accept his offer. I am not angry with him either. I wish I could have been the one to make a happy family with him."

Jochebed squirms uncomfortably and repositions the baby on her lap. "I know it must have been hard for you to see the opportunity to make your own family slip away."

"Thank you. Also, I want to tell you I didn't go with my mother when she went to tell my brothers about your new baby. She knew they would tell the Egyptians. I told her it was wrong to report the baby, but she would not listen to me. She never listens to me. There was nothing I could do about it. Uh…I am sorry the Egyptians came to take your child. You must have been terrified. I am glad they did not take him. I would be very sad. I am ashamed that my mother and brothers reported him to Pharaoh's soldiers."

Surprised, Jochebed raises her eyebrows. "Thank you for that. I never thought you had any good thoughts for me, my mother, or my children."

"Um, ah, well," Orpha stammers, "I never disliked you. I know none of the bad things that happened in our family were your fault. I'm sorry we could not get to know each other. I always wanted a sister. I watched you and wished I could talk with you and your friends."

After a long pause to gather her thoughts, Jochebed says, "I also wish it could have been different, but your mother and your brothers would not allow it. We never had any chance to talk to each other."

Orpha twists her hands nervously. "Uh. I know. But things have changed. Uh. Ah. It is different now. Maybe things will be different."

The young mother looks at Orpha. "How are things different now?"

"I have moved into Father's house." She waits to see Jochebed's reaction.

Jochebed leans forward with rapt attention.

Orpha continues. "Soldiers came five days ago and took my brothers and my mother. They are confined to prison! Mother thought they would get a good reward for reporting a baby, but for some reason, Pharaoh became very angry. I do not know why Pharaoh's soldiers came and arrested them. It may have had something to do with reporting your baby."

Jochebed's mouth drops open. Her eyes widen as she tries to comprehend what she just heard. It is her turn to stammer over her words as many more questions come to mind.

"Uh. Umm. Oh. Thank you for telling me this, Orpha. I am grateful to you. I know this took courage, and you have courage. I admire you for your courage."

"Thank you, Jochebed, but I do not feel courageous. I was too ashamed to tell Father about your baby. If he knew my mother and brothers betrayed your family, he may not recover from the grief. All he knows is they made the Egyptians angry. Father said I should come to live in his house. He suspects I am not telling him all the truth, but I can't tell him about the baby."

"Orpha, I am happy to know you refused to have any part in reporting my baby. I am glad you admit telling the Egyptians about his birth was wrong. Thank you for sparing my father much pain." Jochebed idly toys with the baby as she listens to Orpha continue her speech.

Orpha lowers her head and keeps her eyes on the floor as if contemplating the woven patterns on the rug where she is sitting. "When Mother said she was going to my brothers to tell them about your baby after she promised Mahala she would not tell, that was all I could take. All my life I have tried to please Mother, but I could not live the rest of my life knowing a baby would die because I was too afraid to say 'no' to my mother. I have lived with that fear of saying 'no' to Mother for much too long. I want to make a new life."

Jochebed looks up toward Orpha and says," It takes courage to determine to make a new life. You are showing courage. What are you going to do to make this new life?"

Orpha's face takes on a more pleasant look. Her eyes lift, erasing some of her sour expression.

"I decided to start at Father's house by getting to know Hogla. I learned your mother is a very good woman. She listens when I talk to her. She is very sweet. I help her with Father's needs. Caring for a sick person is very hard, and she seems grateful for my help."

Genuinely touched Jochebed says, "Yes. My mother is a very good woman. She is lonely much of the time, so she must enjoy your company."

Orpha measures her speech and tries not to stumble over her words. "I did not tell her about your baby. I do not want her to hate me or be angry with me for going with Mother when she tricked Aaron into letting us come into your house. I have lived too many years with anger and hate. I cannot live that way any longer."

Jochebed says nothing. She sits toying with her child's hands. She is lost in her own thoughts until Orpha breaks the silence.

"There is something else I want to ask of you."

"Yes. What is it?"

"Umm. Ah… May I call you, Uh…. 'Sister'?"

Minutes pass before Jochebed answers. For the first time, she sees her half-sister from a different perspective. Orpha is not as she always imagined: a bitter, mean-spirited person who wishes harm and hardship on others. Instead, she is a sad, lonely young woman who all her life has struggled with the conflict between a bitter, self-centered, overbearing mother, and a devoutly religious father who goes to great lengths to avoid confrontation with his wife.

Jochebed's own words hit her with stinging force. "I hate Orpha, too! I wish they were dead!" Shame and remorse stab her conscience. She feels her face flushed with shame and embarrassment.

The young mother looks up toward the ceiling and draws in a deep breath. She closes her eyes tight to keep back tears. Mahala's words ring in her ears, "Anger and hatred are heavy burdens-much too heavy to carry. They must be put aside."

"I will consider that, Orpha. Yes. I will consider that. Yes. You are my sister," she whispers softly.

Orpha's face breaks into a rare smile that lights her eyes, lifting the deep creases of sadness that pull her face into a pucker. Suddenly she is transformed into a more attractive woman. "I am happy I came. Thank you, Sister."

Jochebed returns a hesitant smile. "Will you tell our father I love him? Amram and I will bring the children to visit all of you when we are sure it is safe."

"I will tell him. He will be happy." Orpha gets up and stands looking down at Jochebed. "I must go now. Thank you for hearing me."

Orpha wipes her eyes on her sleeve. She awkwardly takes a step toward

Jochebed as if unsure of what she should do. She stoops and gently kisses Jochebed on the forehead. "Thank you, Sister. Thank you."

Jochebed says softly, "Go in peace, Sister. We will talk again soon."

Later in the evening after Amram returns home and learns about Pharaoh's orders to arrest his uncles and Abahail, he acts quickly to contact his most trusted sources of information to learn the reasons for the arrest. His informants, some of whom work in the Pharaoh's palace, interview their witnesses and validate the story.

Within a week they report back with their complete findings of the events that occurred.

The final report was that Amram's uncles contacted the Egyptian military commander. They told the commander that Amram was disobeying Pharaoh's commands by hiding a child.

They further said that Amram was a violent man who was planning an uprising.

When the commander came for the child, he saw Pharaoh's insignia on the bracelet. He became alarmed and decided to check out the bracelet before proceeding with the mission.

The commander then learned about the princess's plan to adopt the baby. To clear himself of any blame, he reported Abahail's sons to Pharaoh saying they deceived him when they reported the baby. He had no prior notice that any baby was exempt from Pharaoh's order. He pleaded that he was just following the commands as Pharaoh had issued them.

When the princess learned that her soon-to-be adopted son came so close to losing his life, she was furious. Determined no one else would attempt to harm the child, she demanded all involved in the scheme be punished severely.

Pharaoh did not want to lose a good military commander. He agreed the commander's story was logical, so the commander was allowed to go free. But to pacify his distraught daughter and her mother, the king ordered all others who were involved in the incident to be confined to prison until further notice.

Still not satisfied, Pharaoh's daughter, with the help of her mother, demanded that her father rescind the order to kill male Hebrew children. Pharaoh agreed. With this, the princess was satisfied.

Amram, to be sure of the accuracy of the report, contacted some of the key witnesses himself. He was especially interested in whether the command to kill the Hebrew children was rescinded. To his relief, he found this to be true. The brutal command was suspended until further notice.

Two days after he received the report, Amram went to Benaiah and several of his most trusted men. He asked them to go throughout the villages before dawn sounding the shofar and announce a meeting to be held at the Place of the Palms that evening after the workday's ends.

The people gather under the palm trees according to their rank. The standard of the tribe is posted. Amram, with Benaiah sitting at his right hand, stands tall on the high cliff and addresses the crowd in a steady, strong voice, clear enough for all to hear.

"My dear brothers, this day like all our days has been long and hard. I know you feel tired and ready for some rest just as I am feeling. Your pain is my pain. I know the agony of wounds from the lash of a taskmaster's whip. My back and my arms are scarred with these lash marks." He holds up his arms so the scars can be clearly seen.

"Like you, when I wake up in the morning, I often wonder if I will return home to see my wife and children, or will I lie dead under a massive rock intended to grace an idol's temple? Worry is our constant companion. It never leaves us. Rest often eludes us. We cannot be sure what a day will bring."

He pauses and watches the people who are looking at him with rapt attention.

"As our lives get harder every day. Evil seems to be coming on us more and more. Our losses are multiplying as more of our children are lost. Many of us are wondering, where is our God? Where is this Almighty

God, who we are told, did wonderful deeds for our fathers? Is he hearing our cries? Why has he not spoken to us? Why has he not acted? Questions such as these are constantly on our mind."

Again, he pauses to gauge the response of the people. All eyes are focused on him. They are leaning forward hanging on to every word.

"Over a year ago my wife let me know she was with child. I started to dread the birth since I knew if the child was a boy, I would lose him. I would know the lasting grief so many of you are experiencing over the loss of your sons."

He makes a signal with his hand to tell someone to come forward.

A young man steps from behind three men who are standing near Amram. He brings a bundle to Amram. Smiling, Amram unwraps the swaddling and holds the baby up for all to see.

A collective gasp rises from the crowd. They are astonished, asking if this man has lost his reason. They whisper questions, "Why is Amram willing to display his infant son when infants are in mortal danger?" This act seems reckless and foolish.

But Amram speaks loudly, confidently, "Three months ago, he was born as dawn approached. I was holding him up like this for his mother to see him when the sun's rays came through the window. The light from heaven above blessed him as one chosen for an important mission. I believed then as I now believe even more strongly, that he is one who will deliver us. He is the one the Almighty has chosen to rescue his people."

The baby is starting to cry. Amram hands the child back to the young man. All eyes watch as the child is carried to his mother who is sitting on the grass near the palm trees with Mahala, Sarah, and Miriam.

Amram continues his speech.

"For three months we hid him as some of you are hiding your children. No one knew of his birth. By trickery and deceit, some of our own family members discovered our secret and decided to report his birth to the Egyptians."

Groans and shocked cries rise from the crowd. Some exchange knowing glances as if to say, "I know who you are speaking about."

"We were desperate to learn how to save our son. As my wife was praying for answers, a plan came to her. The plan was this. She should weave a basket and make it watertight so it would float in the river. When she finished it, the basket with its lid looked like a little ark." He makes the shape of an ark with his hands.

"She placed the baby in the basket and put the basket in the river at the place where Pharaoh's daughter comes to bathe. Pharaoh's daughter found the basket and decided to adopt our son as her own. She hired my wife to nurse our son until he is weaned."

Sounds of shock arise from the assembly. They look at each other and then at Amram as if to say, "How can this be true?"

Amram lowers his head for a minute. He closes his eyes to prevent being overcome with emotion. When he looks up, he says resolutely, "Who can know the plans of the Almighty? His mind is beyond our understanding. The Almighty has his reasons for all his work."

"We will have to give up our son. For this we are sad, but it is for your blessing. Since Pharaoh's daughter intends to adopt our son, she wants to protect him therefore, she persuaded her father to rescind his command to destroy Hebrew sons."

The congregation reacts with a gasp for the second time. Some women burst into weeping. Others excitedly ask each other, "Can this be true? I can't believe it! This is too good to be true!"

When the people calm Amram speaks, "This can only be an act of the Almighty. How strange it all has become! The very river that became the grave for so many and would have swallowed up so many more was the same river where our tiny child was saved."

"Our son's mission has already begun. Because of him, your sons will live. Now you may understand that the Almighty is already using our son to rescue Abraham's children. Because of him, your newborn sons will not be sought out to be murdered. Those who are hiding children may rest from their fear. At least for a little while, we will have some peace. Thanks to our Mighty God!"

The people stand and raise their hands toward heaven. Shouts of praise and thanksgiving rise to the skies. "We give praise and honor to our God! The Almighty be praised! Praise to the God of our fathers who remembers His people! We are his people! Let His people praise him forever! The Lord shall reign forever and ever!"

Chapter 17:
Preparing For A New Adventure

"Fix these words of mine in your hearts and minds; tie them as reminders on your hands and bind them on your foreheads. Teach them to your children, speaking about them when you sit at home and when you walk along the road, when you lie down and when you get up. Write them on the doorposts of your houses and on your gates,..."

Deut. 11:18-20

As life settles into a cautious new normal, Jochebed is determined to make the most of the remaining time with her youngest child. She sets about her task with resolve. The young mother greets each day as an opportunity to enjoy her children, to teach and prepare the youngest child and his siblings for his coming journey to another life.

Every minute must be savored and treasured to make memories and implant lessons into the young minds. She knows the dreaded day of parting will come soon, but she dwells on it only to spur her to additional fervor to make preparations.

At dusk when those who work in the fields return home, the evening meal is finished and the air is cooling, Jochebed gathers her children in the rear courtyard, near the clay oven. She uses this time before retiring for the night as a time of instruction.

"Little Brother will go to live with the princess. He will be a great prince someday when he grows to be a man. He may help us be free from the Egyptians. That will be a happy day. We will live free to do the things we want to do, not what the Egyptians want us to do."

Miriam expresses her doubts. "The princess has a lot of gold and many other nice things. She will give gifts to Little Brother. She will allow him to ride on the boats, and do anything he wants to do. What if he likes boats and all the other things he will get to do? Will he forget about us? If he wants to be like the Egyptians, will he be mean like them? He may not care about us anymore. He will be a prince. Why would he want to remember us?"

"He will not forget. He will remember because he is your brother. You must help him remember by singing your songs to him and telling him stories about the things you learned from Grandmother Mahala. You are a good singer and storyteller. You can help him remember us."

Mahala nods smiling, "I will tell you stories about the great fathers, Abraham, Isaac, and Jacob their wives and children. You can learn even more about the faithful people who trusted the great God. Our God will help him remember us. You must listen carefully."

The children sit listening carefully to the stories about family history, but their favorite stories are about when Aaron was saved from Pharaoh's wrath by hiding in the grain basket and Little Brother was saved by hiding in the floating ark.

When it is deemed safe and Kohath is healthy again, Amram and his family gather in Kohath's courtyard to present the new baby to his great-grandfather. Amram prepares Kohath by explaining to him all that had happened at the birth of his youngest son. The story of how it came about that he would be adopted by Pharaoh's household, brought shouts of praise to the Almighty from the old patriot. The good news about the baby renews his strength and hope for the future of his tribe.

Jochebed kneels close to her esteemed father and gently holds her youngest son for him to see. Miriam and Aaron kneel beside their mother while Amram, Sarah, Mahala, and Hogla stand nearby.

The patriarch's frail, cool hand extends and rests lightly on the child's head. He feels the child's soft hair and smiles. His vision has grown dimmer. He cannot see the baby clearly. Physically he is growing weaker, but his faith continues to grow stronger each day.

"The Lord has blessed me this day. He has allowed me to see the one who will save us. I am resting my hand on the one appointed to save his people. This child is our hope. May the Lord bless him with a strong and brave heart. May the Lord lead him safely through the many, many trials he will face on his long journey." Kohath looks at Jochebed and smiles.

"And I pray the Lord will bless you, sweet mother, that you may help him to grow into a mighty leader for his people. You are a courageous woman and faithful servant. May the Lord bless all your work and give you comfort as you prepare this child for his mission. You have done a very unselfish thing for your family and all the Israelite nation. Your memory will never leave our people."

Jochebed is thrilled to hear her father's blessing.

With the truest sincerity, she says, "Thank you, Father. Your words calm my doubts and fears. I know that I must prepare him for his long journey. I will use every minute I have with him to help him on his very important mission. Our family will help him remember his people even when he is not with us."

Amram says, "Grandfather, may we ask a favor from you?"

Puzzled, Kohath says, "Ask anything you wish. I will do anything I am able to do for you and your family."

Amram states his request. "I know that from the time you were a small boy, you memorized all the history that happened to the ancient peoples of the world. You know the generations that reach back farther than our father Abraham. You remember the legends that were passed down through generations all the way back to Adam, who was the first man created by the Almighty God. My sincere request is that you teach my children all you know about these stories. Will you do this for me and for our people?"

Taken aback, Kohath thinks about this request for a few minutes. He contemplates the enormity of the task. Finally, he says, "If you will help me review the history, I will do as you say. I am honored to do this for you and your family. This history must be kept in the hearts and minds of our people. It must never be forgotten. If I can help with this, I must do it."

"Is it possible to do this great mission? There are so many things that oppose us," Jochebed says doubtfully.

"You ask if this mission is possible when you did the impossible by daring to defy a king who had condemned your baby to death?" Amram smiles and shakes his head. "I know at times we all forget where our real power is. Yes. I believe it is possible. We are not going to do this by ourselves."

He turns toward his grandfather. "I will help you review. I know you will remember everything when you start to relate the stories."

"Miriam and Aaron, will you listen and learn from your grandfather?"

"Yes! Yes!" Miriam dances up and down. "I want to hear the stories I can teach them to Little Brother! He will learn too."

"I want to listen, too. I already know some stories that Grandmother Mahala has taught me. I want to hear more!" Aaron joins Miriam dancing as his eyes sparkle with excitement.

"These children will keep alive this history, and they will remember all its blessings," Kohath smiles. "These young ones are the tribe's hope for Israel's future."

The new assignment for Kohath gives him a new lease on life. The light returns to his eyes and his face is brighter as he relates the stories to the children with a sense of urgency for the message.

He especially emphasizes stories about how the Almighty God cares for His people as they struggle against the temptation and oppression of the evil one. The children sit spellbound with wide eyes. They can fully relate to the concept and often request these stories repeatedly.

Jochebed and Amram watch with pride to see Miriam and Aaron are progressing so well. At first, Little Brother sits in Miriam's lap, and it appears that he is hearing little, yet as soon as he can speak understandable words, it becomes apparent he has understood much of what was said. He quickly learns to relate simple versions of the histories in the correct order.

After several months of learning, Mahala comes out of the house and finds Miriam in the courtyard. "What are you doing with that mud, Miriam? You are using a good pottery jar to hold that muddy water. We do not have jars to spare. You may not be able to get that jar clean. We cannot afford to use our jars for playing in the mud."

Miriam's hands are black with mud splattered up to her elbows. Balls of sticky mud are lined up in rows. She dips her hands in the pottery jar of muddy water.

"Why did you bring that mud in the courtyard?" Mahala says in an annoyed voice.

"I'm making people." Miriam points to two sculpted mud figures that are drying in the sun. "See I made Adam and Eve. Next, I will make Cain and Abel. After that, I'm going to make Noah and all the animals."

Mahala looks at the mud figures. She is amazed that they are so creatively sculpted. "I see. Those mud people you made are very good. How did you learn to make people from mud?"

"The Egyptians make pottery people and animals from clay. I will make them from mud and dry them in the sun. We make bricks from mud, so I can make people and animals from mud as well. Aaron and Brother like playing with the people and animals when I tell them the stories."

Mahala smiles. She was at first frustrated that Miriam was getting mud everywhere. Suddenly she is awed by the girl's creativity and her talent for teaching.

"You are a very good teacher, Miriam. Your brothers will learn many lessons from you. How can they forget any of your lessons? Now I know for sure they will remember."

Chapter 18:
The Final Journey

"He who observes the wind will not sow, and he who regards the clouds will not reap. As you do not know what is the way of the wind, or how the bones grow in the womb of her who is with child, so you do not know the works of God who makes everything."

Ecclesiastes 11:4-5

When the sun rises above the horizon, it gives no hint the long-dreaded day has arrived. After the men have left for the fields, a chariot suddenly appears at the gate. Without ceremony the commander orders the baby must be taken to the river by noon. The princess will take him to Pharaoh's Great House.

An armed Egyptian soldier steps out of the chariot to wait at the house while Jochebed readies the boy for the walk to the bathing place. The soldier will accompany the mother and child as they make their way along the river to the boat.

Even though Jochebed has thought many, many times about this inevitable day, she is not emotionally prepared for it. The sight of the chariot makes her legs weak and her heartbreak. But she must not show strong emotion for fear the Egyptian soldier will seize the boy, and take him away from her by force. She answers softly and respectfully when she receives the order.

The child was allowed to nurse until he had physically developed his immune system and his digestive system enough to allow him to safely eat more substantial food. Babies are often nursed for three or more years. Weaning too early can often result in life-threatening illness. It is not safe for a child to be separated from his mother's milk too early. The princess is taking no chances that the change of diet will harm the young child, so she allows extra time for him to mature. It has been four years since the boy was placed in the little ark. He has grown into a bright, cheerful, winsome young boy.

The soldier, the boy and his mother slowly make their way down the path toward the bathing place. Little Brother walks by his mother's side holding her hand. To calm her troubled heart, Jochebed makes cheerful conversations in Hebrew with her son, hoping the Egyptian does not speak the language. She watches the man out of the corner of her eye to determine if he understands anything she is saying. Egyptians who work with Hebrews on labor projects usually learn enough of the Hebrew language to know what is being said, but many others do not want any association with the Hebrew people; therefore, they do not want to learn what they consider an inferior language.

As she trudges down the path, Jochebed says to her son, "When you were a very small baby, you sailed in a little boat. A royal princess found you floating in the little ark. Now it is time for you to sail in the boat to the Great House. You will see many wonderful things. You will grow to be a strong and mighty prince."

She pauses to see if there is any change of expression on the face of the Egyptian. His face remains expressionless.

"Today you will ride in the big boat. You will breeze through the water very fast. You will go so fast you will feel as if you are swimming like the river ducks. You will have fun." She makes motions of sailing in a boat and swimming like a duck.

Little Brother looks at her with big wide eyes. "I go in the boat?"

"Yes," she nods.

"I go in the boat. Go boat." He makes motions as if he is rowing. "Splish. Splish." He pretends to hit the water with an oar. "Boats go fast. Go fast, boat!"

The soldier shows a slight sign of amusement seeing the boy

pretending to row a boat.

Remembering the song sung by her family in times of trouble, Jochebed starts to sing softly.

"The Lord is my strength and my song. He has become my salvation. He is my God, and I will praise him. My father's God and I will exalt him."

The words take on a more intense meaning of reassurance she has not felt before. "Will you sing this for me?" she asks her son.

Little Brother sings along loudly, even though he has difficulty with the words. She is forced to laugh at his amusing attempts to sing the hard words. Tears sting her eyes. She wipes them with her shawl, grateful to laugh. Laughter keeps back the tears.

As they near the bathing place, she feels she must give her son a blessing even if she is taking a risk with the soldier who may understand what she is saying. If it makes him angry, he may demand that she leave immediately.

The young mother addresses her son softly, but seriously. "When you are living in the Great House, you will grow to be a strong and mighty prince. It may be hard at first, but you will do very well. I know you will do well. Remember the Lord Almighty. The Lord will be at your side to help you in any trouble. The Lord saved Aaron. The Lord saved you as well. You will come back to help your people. The Lord will stay with you and guide you. Every day I will pray to the Lord to help you. When you have trouble, always remember I am praying for you."

The boy looks at her briefly. She risks giving him one last hug before they reach their destination.

The colorful cedar boat is already on shore when they arrive at the appointed place. Titi comes and takes the boy's hand. She leads him toward the stone bench where Meryt sits waiting.

"I am so happy to see you. Look what I brought for you. It is a toy boat. Do you like it?" the princess asks as she shows him a toy boat.

Little Brother takes the toy. His face breaks into a smile of charming innocence. He nods enthusiastically.

"Today you will ride with me in my boat. Won't that be fun? Are you ready to go in the big boat? You will like the boat."

Excited, the young boy smiles and nods with anticipation.

The princess addresses Jochebed. "You have done a very good job nursing my child, and I am happy with your work. Here is your last payment and a bonus as well. I wish you good fortune."

With those words, the princess dismisses the young mother with a wave of her hand and turns her attention back to the boy. Titi hands Jochebed a leather pouch containing money.

Choking down the lump in her throat, Jochebed takes the pouch. She looks at the ground. Desperately she longs to clasp her son to her breast and run away with him as fast as she ran with Aaron that terrible day when Aaron was in danger of losing his life. But she cannot hide this child from the all-seeing eye of the hawk. He must be hidden in plain sight, or he and many other children will be devoured.

Restraining herself, she turns away and pulls her shawl close to her face so no one will notice the tears welling up in her eyes and spilling down her cheeks. Slowly, quietly, she heads toward the village and does not look back.

She has made her preparations as best she knew how, but she wonders if her efforts were enough instruction for so young a child to remember his birth family when he will grow up in a completely different world. Has she done the right thing?

As Fazel holds the boat steady, Titi takes the child by the hand and leads him to the edge of the water. She lifts him into the craft and helps him to a special seat under the canopy.

"You can ride in this little seat made just for you. Won't this be fun? See the big river," Titi says. "Are you ready to go?"

Perched on the seat, the boy enjoys a panoramic view of the great river.

He smiles with a child's delight. The sounds of the waves lapping gently against the craft, the gentle cool breeze ruffling his hair, the smells of the willows and the water—these wonderful new experiences add to his exuberant joy and anticipation of an exciting adventure.

"Go boat. Go, boat. Go!" He bounces in the seat. In his excitement, he does not notice his mother has left the scene.

When all are aboard the craft pulls away from the shore. The princess cannot contain her joy and she laughs giddily.

"Oh, how wonderful! I mourned for years because I had no son. I had no children to comfort me. I was a desolate woman. Now thanks to the great gods of the river I have a son! The gods understood my plight and helped me. They gave me a son!"

She puts her fingertips to her lips and blows a kiss to the river. Her hands go up in a gesture of triumph. "At last! I have a child! My sorrow has been taken away. I found him in the river. I took him from the water. Because he is now truly my son, I will call him Moses!"

Epilogue

"The Lord executes righteousness and justice for all who are oppressed. He made known His ways to Moses, His acts to the children of Israel."

Psalms 103: 6-7

When Moses arrived at the Great House, he was treated as a royal son on his way to becoming a Prince in the Egyptian monarchy. As soon as he was of age, he was immediately enrolled in his schooling where he became a brilliant and diligent student.

His studies included lessons about world history, science, astronomy, mathematics, literature, writing, and military strategy. He traveled to neighboring lands where he learned additional languages and political negotiations. Among the best and the brightest of students, he was preparing to be a player in the upper-class lifestyle of the most powerful and advanced nation in the world at that time.

Strong and agile physically, he excelled in athletics. His companions esteemed him for his humble, winsome characteristics; thus, he got along well with his classmates. From the outside appearances, all seemed to be progressing very well according to Pharaoh's daughter's plan for her adopted son. The Egyptians considered Moses to be a very fortunate youth who was rescued from the drudgery of slavery and transported to a life of luxury where he would enjoy the best the world had to offer.

Yet, all was not well with Moses. There were those frequent times when some recollection, memory, or impression would jog his memory, recalling those brief years of early childhood with his Israelite family in the village. Sometimes it was the sight of an Israelite man working on building projects, a remembered phrase from a song, or a prayer, or the sight of a basket woven by an Israelite woman. Other times it could have been the smell of barley bread cooking in a clay pot. These things aroused dim remnants of memories from his past life. There were times he longed to go back to the village and visit with his family.

Other times he clearly recalled his immediate family and grandparents. He was aware they blessed him and told him he had a great mission. Exactly how this mission was to be accomplished he was not sure.

When Moses became a man, he realized all the magnificent buildings, decorated walls, gardens, and beautiful fountains were built by Israelite people and other slaves who were forced to risk their lives and health to provide opulent living standards for the ruling royalty. These injustices wore on his mind.

Ideas, memories, and feelings were smoldering inside his heart like embers lying beneath a bed of fine, white ashes waiting for that exact gust of wind to blow away the powder, fan the ashes, and drop a wad of straw on the bed of coals to ignite a flame that would become a raging fire.

That gust of wind came one ordinary day as Moses was inspecting one of the building sites. He came upon an Egyptian beating a Hebrew worker. The flame of his heart ignited into anger. He killed the cruel Egyptian. This was his defining moment. He had made his choice. Despite all the careful training he received at the Egyptian schools, the vast wealth, popularity, and power he could have enjoyed, he was not an Egyptian. At that moment the dye was cast. He chose to be a Hebrew.

He buried the body of the Egyptian, hoping and assuming no one saw what happened. But the next day as he walked around the site, he happened upon two Hebrew men quarreling with each other. Moses said to the instigator of the quarrel, "Why are you hitting your brother, Hebrew?"

The man answered impudently, "Who made you a prince and a judge over us? Are you going to kill me as you did with the Egyptian yesterday?"

Shocked, Moses assumed his people would understand he was able to help them. He thought they should know that he had chosen to be on their side. Instead, it appeared they assumed his loyalty was with Pharaoh.

Because of his act of violence, they assumed he had become a cruel Egyptian just like the taskmasters who continually mistreated Israelites for Pharaoh's benefit.

This man's insolent comments were proof to Moses that the murder was not a secret. Pharaoh was aware of the death of the Egyptian. If not, it was just a short time before it would come to his attention. Egyptian soldiers would be coming for him. His life was in immediate danger. There was only one course of action.

With no time to prepare for a journey, Moses ran for his life with very few provisions. Crossing the border into the desert land of Midian, he was no longer a privileged prince. Henceforth, he would be considered a murderer and a fugitive fleeing from the law and justice.

The sparsely occupied country of Midian was primarily inhabited by other fugitives from Pharaoh's wrath—outlaws, bandits, and those especially hardy people who were able to eke out a meager living in wilderness country. To survive, one had to know where to find springs of water in the arid land or depend on the few man-made wells located near small villages.

Moses came to one of these community wells near a remote outpost where shepherds regularly brought their flocks to water. As he sat waiting for a turn at the well, he watched the shepherds watering their flocks. The sheep in one flock were bleating mournfully. These sheep were not getting water. The other flocks were watered and moved on, but this flock did not move into position to receive the water as each group of shepherds took their turn. Soon, Moses understood the problem. The shepherds of this flock were women. The male shepherds took a perverse delight in making the physically weaker female shepherds wait until all male shepherds had finished their watering and moved their sheep from the area. Only then could the women have access to the water for their flock.

Once again Moses' anger was aroused when he witnessed such injustice. He drove away the offending shepherds and then helped the women water their flock. Moses learned these seven sisters were tending the flock of their father, Jethro. Every day they were forced to wait for water and were often harassed and driven away from grazing areas as well. Shepherding was very difficult for young women.

When the sisters arrived home, their father asked how they finished their watering so early. They related the story of the Egyptian who had helped them water their sheep. Jethro, a wise and upright man, told them to go find this Egyptian and invite him to their home as Jethro wished to thank him for his kindness.

Jethro warmly welcomed Moses into his home. When he learned Moses' story, he asked him to stay with them and tend his sheep. No longer a wealthy prince, but an outcast and alone, Moses found a home and family at Jethro's house where he became a lowly shepherd. Moses settled into life with the family. He married Zipporah, Jethro's daughter, and two sons were born from this marriage.

For the next forty years, Moses tended the flocks of Jethro. As he wandered the rocky desert land of Midian day after mundane day, his faith and mental capacities were tested and tried to the limit. Searching for water, grass, and shelter for the large flock of sheep as they moved from place to place familiarized Moses with every inch of the barren territory. These training exercises taught him how to depend upon God's help to survive in a hostile, dangerous environment.

The rigorous life in the wilderness kept his body strong, his eyes sharp, his mental capacities undimmed. Even as he was nearing eighty years of age, he was still a strong and agile man. But by all the world's estimations, he was too old to fulfill the promise of his childhood. It was too late for him to become a great leader. He had lost his political power, his respected position, and his political and social connections. He had nothing with which to help his Israelite people. The sheep were his followers; he was content with his family and the simple life of the desert.

Memories of the dreams his parents long ago related to him, saying he would someday save his people from the enslavement to the Egyptians, became dimmer with each passing day as he grew older. These prophecies spoken in his early childhood by his parents were relegated to the place where childhood dreams are stored when it is assumed they will never be realized.

Yet unknown to him, he was being molded and perfected for his great calling. God had not forgotten his promises to faithful Abraham's family. He was perfecting Moses for his mission. The prophecies were not dead. They were just lying under the ash heap in Moses' heart ready once more to ignite into flame.

This flame was set alight on one fateful day when he encountered God on a barren mountainside. The resulting inferno would radically alter the world's history.

For a brief time, God sent Moses back to Pharaoh's Great House with his brother, Aaron, to plead for the release of his people. When he returned to this barren wilderness he would not be herding sheep. He would be the leader of 600,000 Israelite men and their families.

For forty more years he would wander this barren, rocky wasteland while God patiently molded the freed slaves into a military force that would conquer and reclaim Canaan territory. The sacred land God had promised Father Abraham so long ago would once again be occupied by Abraham's children. Those promises were unshakable. Not one could be nullified. Not one was left unfulfilled, and not one would be broken.

References

Chapter 1. A Solemn Pledge

1. Exodus 2:1. Amram and Jochebed were from the tribe of Levi.
2. Exodus 2:1. Amram took Jochebed, his father's sister, as his wife. *KJV*
3. Exodus 28:1-4. Aaron and his sons were consecrated as priests of God.
4. Genesis 47:11. The Israelites settled in the land of Goshen, the best grazing land in Egypt.
5. Genesis 47:27. The Israelites prospered in Egypt in the early years.
6. Psalms 41:13. Blessed is the Lord God of Israel.
7. Genesis 24:60. Rebekah's blessing for her marriage.
8. Genesis 24:22. Rebekah's bracelet was given to her by Abraham's servant when he met her at a well.
9. Genesis 12:1-3. God's promise to Abraham. God directed Abraham to look at the stars when he pronounced his covenant with Abraham.
10. Genesis 15:8-18. God's covenant with Abraham.
11. Genesis 41:33-57. Joseph became ruler over Egypt.
12. Exodus 1:8-14. Pharaoh forced the people to work in fields and build cities.
13. The Israelites were in Egypt for four hundred and thirty years.

Chapter 2. The Magical Experience

1. *Ancient Egypt.* Hermes House 2002 Annas Publishing Inc. 27 West 20th, New York, NY pg. 409. The Scarab beetle symbolizes the god Khepri, a symbol of life and resurrection, according to the ancient Egyptian myth.

Chapter 3. The Priest, the Pharaoh, and their Plot

1. Lucy Lamy, Egyptian Mysteries. P. 14 (Art and Imagination series, Thames and Hudson, 1981). Kephir represents the scarab beetle as well

as the idea of becoming. Khepri is the entity embodied in the sun as it rises, when darkness becomes light.

2. *Ancient Egypt.* George Hart. Dorling Kindersley Publishing Inc. 375 Hudson Street, New York. New York 1024 p. 342. Horus, the falcon symbolized the king and his all-seeing characteristics.

3. *Ancient Egypt.* George Hart. Dorling Kindersley Publishing Inc. 375 Hudson Street, New York, New York 1024 p. 30. Description of Egyptian priest rituals.

4. Exodus 1:8. The Pharaoh did not know about Joseph because all history of him had been erased or forgotten.

5. Genesis 37:26-28. Joseph is sold into slavery.

6. Genesis 39:6-18. Joseph is accused of attacking Potiphar's wife.

7. Exodus 1:9-11. The Israelites were conscripted into forced labor.

8. Exodus 1:12. The Hebrew people increased in number so the Egyptians feared them.

9. Genesis 42:1-5. Jacob's sons go to Egypt to buy grain.

10. Genesis 46:1-7. Jacob's family goes to Egypt.

11. Genesis 41:1-25. Pharaoh's dreams.

12. Genesis 41:25-32. Joseph interprets Pharaoh's dreams.

13. Genesis 41:37-44. Joseph is made vizier of Egypt.

14. Genesis 41:48-49. Joseph stores grain in preparation for famine.

15. Genesis 41:45. Joseph's Egyptian name.

16. Genesis 47:20. Joseph buys all the land in Egypt for Pharaoh.

17. Genesis 47:22. The Egyptian priesthood retains their land.

18. Genesis 47:27. The Israelites were allowed to live in the rich grazing land of Goshen.

19. Genesis 50:25-26. Joseph's coffin remained with his people to be taken back to Canaan when the people returned to the promised land of Canaan.

20. Genesis 17:1-8. God swore he would give the land of Canaan to Abraham and his descendants.

Chapter 4. The Dreadful Proposition

1. *Ancient Lives, Daily Life in Egypt of the Pharaohs.* John Romer 1984 Holt, Rinehart and Winston, 383 Madison Avenue, New York, New York 1008-p. 53. An Egyptian song.

2. Genesis 43:32. Egyptians considered it an abomination to eat with Hebrews.

3. Exodus 1:15-16 Shiphrah and Purah are commanded to kill the male children as they are born.

Chapter 5. Prejudice, Doubt, and Fear

1. Genesis 46:34. Shepherds were an abomination to the ancient Egyptians.

2. Genesis 12:15. The Egyptian Pharaoh takes Sarah for himself.

3. Genesis 18:10. God promises Sarah a son.

4. Genesis 18:11-15. Sarah hears the promise but she does not believe at first.

5. Genesis 21:1-3. Sarah gives birth to the child.

Chapter 6. The Late-Night Tragedy

1. Ancient childbirth seat found in Egypt: Blueyonder. Http://www.ancienthistorypwp.blue yonder.com.uk/enter/news272htmlhttp 04 Nov. 2002. Women gave birth sitting on a brick birthing chair with a hole in the bottom.

2. Parsons, Marie, "Childbirth and children in Ancient Egypt." Tour Egypt. Http://www.touregypt.netfeaturesstories/mothers.htm. Childbirth in ancient Egypt was very risky for the child and its mother.

Chapter 7. Unwitting Collaboration

2. Ecclesiastes 7:13. Consider the work of God.

3. Exodus 1:17. Shiphrah and Puah did not obey Pharaoh's command.

4. Exodus 1:18-19. The midwives said the Hebrew women were too strong and did not need assistance from the midwives; therefore, they could not

get to the birthing mother soon enough to kill the male children.

5. Exodus 1:20-21. God blessed the midwives and protected them because they refused to obey Pharaoh's commands.

Chapter 8. Red Paint on the Gate and a Soothsayer's Warning

1. Ancient Lives, Daily Life in Egypt of the Pharaohs. John Romer, 1984. Holt, Rinehart and Winston. 383 Madison Avenue, New York, New York. An Egyptian song.

Chapter 9. The Unholy Sacrifice and the Horrific Day of Sorrow

2. Jeremiah 31:15. Jeremiah alludes to the slaughter of Israelite children in the Babylonian captivity. Jeremiah is quoted at Jesus' birth.

3. Matthew 2:16-18 Herod, like Pharaoh, destroyed the male Israelite children two years old and under.

Chapter 10. The Prophecy and a Message from the Starry Sky.

1. Psalms 71:4-6. In times of trouble call upon the Lord.

2. Genesis 15:13-16. Abraham's children would be slaves in a foreign land.

3. Genesis 15:13. Abraham's children would be slaves for 400 years.

4. Genesis 15:14. God will lead the people out of the land with great possessions.

5. Genesis 15:14. God will judge the nation that enslaved Abraham's children.

6. Genesis 15:16-18. The covenant with Abraham was sealed with a blood oath. The blood of animals, a heifer, a goat, a ram and a dove and a pigeon, served as the sacrifice.

7. Genesis 15:17. A smoking pot and a burning torch, each a symbol of God, walked the trail of blood signifying God's acceptance of the covenant.

8. Genesis 49:24. Jacob's blessing is the first recorded reference to God as a Shepherd to his people.

9. Psalms 44:22. God's people are regarded as sheep to be slaughtered.

10. Romans 8:35-36. The apostle Paul quotes Psalm 44:22. The slaughtered

ones are considered conquerors.

11. Revelations 6:9. Those slain for the Word of God are shown as "under the altar," or as sacrifices, offerings, for the cause of Christ.

12. Psalms 148:3. The heavenly bodies and stars praise God.

13. Psalms 8:3. The heavens and stars show the glory of God.

14. Psalms 19:1-4. The heavens tell the glory of God to all people on the earth.

Chapter 11. A Divine Blessing and Resolute Determination

1. Isaiah 55:8-9. God's thoughts are higher than men's thoughts.

Chapter 12. The Dismal Princess and an Overheard Conversation

1. Isaiah 45:9-10. God is the true God. There are no others.

Chapter 13. Deception and Discovery

1. Psalms 57:1-2. The Lord fulfills his purpose in individuals.

Chapter 14 The Daring Scheme

2. Psalms 102:18-21. The Lord hears the calls of the helpless.

3. Hebrews 11:23. Amram and Jochebed were not afraid of Pharaoh's command. They decided to defy the king's order and hide their baby.

4. Hebrews 11:23. Amram and Jochebed saw Moses as a special child.

5. Exodus 2:2. Moses was hidden for three months after his birth.

6. Exodus 2:2. Moses was a beautiful child.

7. Exodus 2:3. Moses' mother made a basket of papyrus and made it watertight with tar and pitch.

8. Exodus 2:4. Miriam watched to see what would happen to the basket.

9. Exodus 2:5. Pharaoh's daughter sent her maid to fetch the basket.

10. Exodus 2:5-8. Miriam brings Jochebed to nurse the baby for the princess.

11. Exodus 2:9. The princess hires Jochebed to nurse the baby for her.

Chapter 16. Reconciliation and Preparation

1. Genesis 29:18. Jacob was in love with Rachel and wanted to marry her.

2. Genesis 29:17. Rachel was beautiful. Leah was older but not as beautiful.

3. Genesis 29:23. Laban, father of Rachel and Leah, tricked Jacob by giving him Leah in marriage instead of Rachel.

4. Genesis 29:31, 33. Jacob did not love Leah.

5. Genesis 49:3-4. Reuben, Jacob's oldest son by Leah, showed ultimate contempt for his father when he slept with his father's concubine.

Chapter 17. The Final Journey

1. Jeremiah 29:11-12. The Lord has plans for those who call on him.

2. Parsons, Marie, "Childbirth and Children in Ancient Egypt." Tour Egypt Http://touregypt.netgearturesstories/mothers.htm. Children were nursed for approximately three years in ancient Egypt.

3. Acts 7:23-25. Moses knew, while he was still in Pharaoh's house, God gave him a mission to rescue his people.

4. Exodus 15:2. From the Song of Moses.

5. *The Oxford Annotated Bible. The Holy Bible.* Herbert G. May Y Bruce M. Metzger. New York, Oxford University Press, 1962. "Moses" is the Egyptian word for "son" meaning "to begat a child." Compare "Tut-Mose." In Exodus, it is explained with the Hebrew word "to draw out."

Epilogue

1. Acts 7:22. Moses was well educated in the Egyptian schools. He was mighty in words and deeds.

2. Acts 7:25. Moses thought his people would know God had sent him to deliver them, but they did not understand.

3. Exodus 2:11-24. Moses flees to Midian.

4. Acts 7:29. In the land of Midian Moses had two sons.

5. Acts 7:30. Moses tended Jethro's flocks for forty years.

6. Acts 7:30. Moses met God on Mount Sinai and received his commission to go to Egypt to rescue His Chosen People.

7. Exodus 12:37. Six hundred thousand men and their children left Egypt under Moses' leadership.

Questions for Discussion

1. Chapter 1. God made a promise to Abraham that his descendants would be enslaved for 400 years, and then they would leave with a great victory. This promise was made 500 years before the Israelites left Egypt. Kohath wanted to instill hope in his people by reminding them of the 500-year-old promises made to their ancestors. Do you believe that promises God made through his prophets, apostles, and teachers 2000 to 3000 years in the past are relevant for modern-day believers?

2. Chapter 2. Abahail brought an image of an Egyptian god as a gift for Jochebed's baby. Mahala refused to allow the gift to be given. Was Mahala correct in her objection? How should believers in Jehovah God regard palm reading, or consultation with fortune tellers to determine their future? Should believers in God wear or possess symbols or good luck charms or any other things associated with false religions that promise protection or guidance in making life decisions? Why or why not?

3. Chapter 5. In ancient times child sacrifice was practiced by nearly all nations except Israel. It was an accepted part of the pagan religions. Shiphrah and Puah refused to obey Pharaoh's command to kill male children. Would these two women have been justified in obeying the king's command to save their own lives and those of their families? Would they have been justified in obeying Pharaoh if obedience to the command would bring about a better life for themselves and their families? How did God regard the midwives' decision? Exodus 2:20

4. Chapter 10. Mahala compares the murdered babies to lambs taken from a flock to be slaughtered by the shepherd. She says the lambs are like sacrifices for the rest of the flock. Do you believe children who die before they have lived have a place in God's plan? Why? Why not?

5. Chapter 10. Because God referred to the stars when he made promises to Abraham, Jochebed associated the stars with God's promises. She declares that the promises are like the stars in that they are fixed for all times and cannot be nullified by the unbelief of or behavior of the people. Do you believe changes in social norms or human beliefs alter God's plans or promises from one generation to another?

6. Chapter 14. Amram and Jochebed decided to give up their son to people who believed in a religion hostile to theirs. They did all they knew to do to keep him faithful to the Hebrew beliefs. All three of their children became faithful leaders in God's plan to save the Hebrew people. Do you believe it is possible to instill lasting faith in children despite a culture that is hostile to God in today's world? If so, what is required to accomplish this with your children?

A Note from the Author

This book has been on my mind for many years. When I learned I would give birth to a child, I became interested in Jochebed and wondered how this slave woman could teach her children to be faithful in an environment so adverse to her efforts to raise them according to God's will. How did she keep her own faith under so much pressure?

What happened to prompt this woman to leave her baby in a crocodile-infested river in a basket to be found by a member of the royal family? How could this happen?

Since the information in the Bible about Jochebed and Amram is sketchy, we know very little about this family. To weave a story of this faithful couple, additional fictional characters were added to enhance the narrative.

After researching the lifestyles of ancient peoples of that time, I attempted to make the narrative as interesting and realistic as possible. Any errors you may find are unintentional.

In the construction of this story, I have tried to stay as close as possible to the biblical account. References for all I found recorded about the story and the primary characters are listed to help those who want to do further study.

A big thank you to the many who have encouraged me and helped me in this long struggle to bring the writing of this book to completion.

My husband and children are a constant inspiration and encouragement. Without them, I could not have finished it.

My sister, Alice Banker, was indispensable in helping me stay on course. She is my greatest fan.

Thanks to my large, extended family and many friends who are always ready to offer support for any endeavor. We are a family of faith and encouragement to each other.

And thanks to all parents who have not lost hope and are daily working with their children to ensure their continued walk in the ways of God.

May God's blessings be upon all of you.

www.ingramcontent.com/pod-product-compliance
Lightning Source LLC
LaVergne TN
LVHW040144080526
838202LV00042B/3017